For a moment neither man moved. Then Steve kicked the trombone away from him and squashed the cigarette in a glass tray. His black eyes were empty but his mouth grinned whitely.

"If you want trouble," he said, "I come from where they make it."

Leopardi smiled, thinly, tautly, and his right hand came up out of the suitcase with a gun in it. His thumb snicked the safety catch. He held the gun steady, pointing. "Make some with this," he said, and fired.

# THE SIMPLE ART OF MURDER

contains four stories. The title piece is Chandler's own definitive statement on the art of the mystery story. Nobody has ever improved on it.

"You can't ask for anything better."
　　　　　　　　　　　　—San Francisco Chronicle

Also by Raymond Chandler
*Published by Ballantine Books:*

KILLER IN THE RAIN

THE LITTLE SISTER

THE LONG GOODBYE

PICKUP ON NOON STREET

PLAYBACK

TROUBLE IS MY BUSINESS

# RAYMOND CHANDLER

## THE SIMPLE ART OF MURDER

BALLANTINE BOOKS • NEW YORK

# CONTENTS

# THE SIMPLE ART
# OF MURDER

*An Essay*

FICTION in any form has always intended to be realistic. Old-fashioned novels which now seem stilted and artificial to the point of burlesque did not appear that way to the people who first read them. Writers like Fielding and Smollett could seem realistic in the modern sense because they dealt largely with uninhibited characters, many of whom were about two jumps ahead of the police, but Jane Austen's chronicles of highly inhibited people against a background of rural gentility seem real enough psychologically. There is plenty of that kind of social and emotional hypocrisy around today. Add to it a liberal dose of intellectual pretentiousness and you get the tone of the book page in your daily paper and the earnest and fatuous atmosphere breathed by discussion groups in little clubs. These are the people who make best sellers, which are promotional jobs based on a sort of indirect snob appeal, carefully escorted by the trained seals of the critical fraternity, and lovingly tended and watered by certain much too powerful pressure groups whose business is selling books, although they would like you to think they are fostering culture. Just get a little behind in your payments and you will find out how idealistic they are.

The detective story for a variety of reasons can seldom be promoted. It is usually about murder and hence lacks the element of uplift. Murder, which is a frustration of the individual and hence a frustration of the race, may have, and in fact has, a good deal of sociological implication. But it has been going on too long for it to be news. If the mystery novel is at all realistic (which it very seldom is) it is written in a certain spirit of detachment; otherwise nobody but a psychopath would want to write it or read it. The murder novel has also a depressing way of minding its own business, solving its own problems and answering its own questions. There is nothing left to discuss, except whether it was well enough written to be good fiction, and the people who make up the half-million sales wouldn't know that anyway. The detection of quality in writing is difficult enough even for those who make a career of the job, without paying too much attention to the matter of advance sales.

The detective story (perhaps I had better call it that, since the English formula still dominates the trade) has to find its public by a slow process of distillation. That it does do this, and holds on thereafter with such tenacity, is a fact; the reasons for it are a study for more patient minds than mine. Nor is it any part of my thesis to maintain that it is a vital and significant form of art. There are no vital and significant forms of art; there is only art, and precious little of that. The growth of populations has in no way increased the amount; it has merely increased the adeptness with which substitutes can be produced and packaged.

Yet the detective story, even in its most conventional form, is difficult to write well. Good specimens of the art are much rarer than good serious novels. Second-rate items outlast most of the high-velocity fiction, and a great many that should never have been born simply refuse to die at all. They are as durable as the statues in public parks and just about as dull.

This fact is annoying to people of what is called discernment. They do not like it that penetrating and important works of fiction of a few years back stand on their special shelf in the library marked "Best-sellers of Yesteryear" or something, and nobody goes near them but an occasional shortsighted customer who bends down, peers briefly and hurries away; while at the same time old ladies jostle each other at the mystery shelf to grab off some item of the same vintage with such a title as *The Triple Petunia Murder Case* or *Inspector Pinchbottle to the Rescue*. They do not like it at all that "really important books" (and some of them are too, in a way) get the frosty mitt at the reprint counter while *Death Wears Yellow Garters* is put out in editions of fifty or one hundred thousand copies on the newsstands of the country, and is obviously not there just to say goodbye.

To tell the truth, I do not like it very much myself. In my less stilted moments I too write detective stories, and all this immortality makes just a little too much competition. Even Einstein couldn't get very far if three hundred treatises of the higher physics were published every year, and several thousand others in some form or other were hanging around in excellent condition, and being read too.

Hemingway says somewhere that the good writer competes only with the dead. The good detective story writer (there must after all be a few) competes not only with all the unburied dead but with all the hosts of the living as well. And on almost equal terms; for it is one of the qualities of this kind of writing that the thing that makes people read it never goes out of style. The hero's tie may be a little out of the mode and the good gray inspector may arrive in a dogcart instead of a streamlined sedan with siren screaming, but what he does when he gets there is the same old futzing around with timetables and bits of charred paper and who trampled the jolly old flowering arbutus under the library window.

I have, however, a less sordid interest in the matter. It seems to me that production of detective stories on so large a scale, and by writers whose immediate reward is small and whose meed of critical praise is almost nil, would not be possible at all if the job took any talent. In that sense the raised eyebrow of the critic and the shoddy merchandising of the publisher are perfectly logical. The average detective story is probably no worse than the average novel, but you never see the average novel. It doesn't get published. The average— or only slightly above average—detective story does. Not only is it published but it is sold in small quantities to rental libraries and it is read. There are even a few optimists who buy it at the full retail price of two dollars, because it looks so fresh and new and there is a picture of a corpse on the cover.

And the strange thing is that this average, more than middling dull, pooped-out piece of utterly unreal and mechanical fiction is really not very different from what are called the masterpieces of the art. It drags on a little more slowly, the dialogue is a shade grayer, the cardboard out of which the characters are cut is a shade thinner, and the cheating is a little more obvious. But it is the same kind of book. Whereas the good novel is not at all the same kind of book as the bad novel. It is about entirely different things. But the good detective story and the bad detective story are about exactly the same things, and they are about them in very much the same way. There are reasons for this too, and reasons for the reasons; there always are.

I suppose the principal dilemma of the traditional or classic or straight deductive or logic and deduction novel of detection is that for any approach to perfection it demands a combination of qualities not found in the same mind. The coolheaded constructionist does not also come across with lively characters, sharp dialogue, a sense of pace, and an acute use of observed detail. The grim logician has as much atmosphere as a drawing board. The scientific sleuth has a nice new shiny laboratory, but I'm sorry I can't remember the face. The fellow who can write you a vivid and colorful prose simply will not be bothered with the coolie labor of breaking down unbreakable alibis.

The master of rare knowledge is living psychologically in the age of the hoop skirt. If you know all you should know about ceramics and Egyptian needlework, you don't know anything at all about the police. If you know that platinum won't melt under about 3000° F. by itself, but will melt at the glance of a pair of deep blue eyes if you put it near a bar of lead, then you don't know how men make love in the twentieth century. And if you know enough about the elegant *flânerie* of the pre-war French Riviera to lay your story in that locale, you don't know that a couple of capsules of barbital small enough to be swallowed will not only not kill a man—they will not even put him to sleep if he fights against them.

Every detective story writer makes mistakes, of course, and none will ever know as much as he should. Conan Doyle made mistakes which completely invalidated some of his stories, but he was a pioneer, and Sherlock Holmes after all is mostly an attitude and a few dozen lines of unforgettable dialogue. It is the ladies and gentlemen of what Mr. Howard Haycraft (in his book *Murder for Pleasure*) calls the Golden Age of detective fiction that really get me down. This age is not remote. For Mr. Haycraft's purpose it starts after the First World War and lasts up to about 1930. For all practical purposes it is still here. Two thirds or three quarters of all the detective stories published still adhere to the formula the giants of this era created, perfected, polished, and sold to the world as problems in logic and deduction.

These are stern words, but be not alarmed. They are only words. Let us glance at one of the glories of the literature, an acknowledged masterpiece of the art of fooling the reader without cheating him. It is called *The Red House Mystery*, was written by A. A. Milne, and has been named by Alexander Woollcott (rather a fast man with a superlative) "one of the three best mystery stories of all time." Words of that size are not spoken lightly. The book was published in 1922 but is timeless, and might as easily have been published in July, 1939, or, with a few slight changes, last week. It ran thirteen editions and seems to have been in print, in the original format, for about sixteen years. That happens to few books of any kind. It is an agreeable book, light, amusing in the *Punch* style, written with a deceptive smoothness that is not so easy as it looks.

It concerns Mark Ablett's impersonation of his brother Robert, as a hoax on his friends. Mark is the owner of the Red House, a typical laburnum-and-lodge-gate English country house. He has a secretary who encourages him and abets him in this impersonation, and who is going to murder him if he pulls it off. Nobody around the Red House has ever seen Robert, fifteen years absent in Australia and known by repute as a no-good. A letter is talked about (but never shown) announcing Robert's arrival, and Mark hints it will not be a pleasant occasion. One afternoon, then, the supposed Robert arrives, identifies himself to a couple of servants, is shown into the study. Mark goes in after him (according to testimony at the inquest). Robert is then found dead on the floor with a bullet hole in his face, and of course Mark has vanished into thin air. Arrive the police, who suspect Mark must be the murderer, remove the débris, and proceed with the investigation—and in due course, with the inquest.

Milne is aware of one very difficult hurdle and tries as well as he can to get over it. Since the secretary is going to murder Mark, once Mark has established himself as Robert, the impersonation has to continue and fool the police. Since, also, everybody around the Red House knows Mark intimately, disguise is necessary. This is achieved by shaving off Mark's beard, roughening his hands ("not the hands of a manicured gentleman"—testimony), and the use of a gruff voice and rough manner.

But this is not enough. The cops are going to have the body and the clothes on it and whatever is in the pockets. Therefore none of this must suggest Mark. Milne therefore works like a switch engine to put over the motivation that Mark is such a thoroughly conceited performer that he dresses the part down to the socks and underwear (from all of which the secretary has removed the maker's labels), like a ham blacking himself all over to play Othello. If the reader will buy this (and the sales record shows he must have), Milne figures he is solid. Yet, however light in texture the story may be, it is offered as a problem of logic and deduction.

If it is not that, it is nothing at all. There is nothing else for it to be. If the situation is false, you cannot even accept it as a light novel, for there is no story for the light novel to be about. If the problem does not contain the elements of truth and plausibility, it is no problem; if the logic is an illusion, there is nothing to deduce. If the impersonation is impossible once the reader is told the conditions it must fulfill, then the whole thing is a fraud. Not a deliberate fraud, because Milne would not have written the story if he had known what he was up against. He is up against a number of deadly things, none of which he even considers. Nor, apparently, does the casual reader, who wants to like the story—hence takes it at its face value. But the reader is not called upon to know the facts of life when the author does not. The author is the expert in the case.

Here is what this author ignores:

1. The coroner holds formal jury inquest on a body for which no legal competent identification is offered. A coroner, usually in a big city, will sometimes hold inquest on a body that *cannot* be identified, if the record of such an inquest has or may have a value (fire, disaster, evidence of murder). No such reason exists here, and there is no one to identify the body. Witnesses said the man said he was Robert Ablett. This is mere presumption, and has weight only if nothing conflicts with it. Identification is a condition precedent to an inquest. It is a matter of law. Even in death a man has a right to his own identity. The coroner will, wherever humanly possible, enforce that right. To neglect it would be a violation of his office.

2. Since Mark Ablett, missing and suspected of the murder, cannot defend himself, all evidence of his movements before and after the murder is vital (as also whether he has money to run away on); yet all such evidence is given by the man closest to the murder and is without corroboration. It is automatically suspect until proved true.

3. The police find by direct investigation that Rob-

ert Ablett was not well thought of in his native village. Somebody there must have known him. No such person was brought to the inquest. (The story couldn't stand it.)

4. The police know there is an element of threat in Robert's supposed visit, and that it is connected with the murder must be obvious to them. Yet they make no attempt to check Robert in Australia, or find out what character he had there, or what associates, or even if he actually came to England, and with whom. (If they had, they would have found out he had been dead three years.)

5. The police surgeon examines a body with a recently shaved beard (exposing unweathered skin) and artificially roughened hands, but it is the body of a wealthy, soft-living man, long resident in a cool climate. Robert was a rough individual and had lived fifteen years in Australia. That is the surgeon's information. It is impossible he would have noticed nothing to conflict with it.

6. The clothes are nameless, empty, and have had the labels removed. Yet the man wearing them asserted an identity. The presumption that he was not what he said he was is overpowering. Nothing whatever is done about his peculiar circumstance. It is never even mentioned as being peculiar.

7. A man is missing, a well-known local man, and a body in the morgue closely resembles him. It is impossible that the police should not at once eliminate the chance that the missing man *is* the dead man. Nothing would be easier than to prove it. Not even to think of it is incredible. It makes idiots of the police, so that a brash amateur may startle the world with a fake solution.

The detective in the case is an insouciant amateur named Anthony Gillingham, a nice lad with a cheery eye, a nice little flat in town, and that airy manner. He is not making any money on the assignment, but is always available when the local gendarmerie loses its notebook. The English police endure him with their customary stoicism, but I shudder to think what the boys down at the Homicide Bureau in my city would do to him.

There are even less plausible examples of the art than this. In *Trent's Last Case* (often called "the perfect detective story") you have to accept the premise that a giant of international finance, whose lightest frown makes Wall Street quiver like a chihuahua, will plot his own death so as to hang his secretary, and that the secretary when pinched will maintain an aristocratic silence—the old Etonian in him, maybe. I have known relatively few international financiers, but I rather think the author of this novel has (if possible) known fewer.

There is another one, by Freeman Wills Crofts (the soundest builder of them all when he doesn't get too fancy), wherein a murderer, by the aid of make-up, split-second timing and some very sweet evasive action, impersonates the man he has just killed and thereby gets him alive and distant from the place of the crime. There is one by Dorothy Sayers in which a man is murdered alone at night in his house by a mechanically released weight which works because he always turns the radio on at just such a moment, always stands in just such a position in front of it, and always bends over just so far. A couple of inches either way and the customers would get a rain check. This is what is vulgarly known as having God sit in your lap; a murderer who needs that much help from Providence must be in the wrong business.

And there is a scheme of Agatha Christie's featuring

M. Hercule Poirot, that ingenious Belgian who talks in a literal translation of school-boy French. By duly messing around with his "little gray cells" M. Poirot decides that since nobody on a certain through sleeper could have done the murder alone, everybody did it together, breaking the process down into a series of simple operations like assembling an egg beater. This is the type that is guaranteed to knock the keenest mind for a loop. Only a halfwit could guess it.

There are much better plots by these same writers and by others of their school. There may be one somewhere that would really stand up under close scrutiny. It would be fun to read it, even if I did have to go back to page 47 and refresh my memory about exactly what time the second gardener potted the prize-winning tea-rose begonia. There is nothing new about these stories and nothing old. The ones I mentioned are all English because the authorities, such as they are, seem to feel that the English writers had an edge in this dreary routine and that the Americans, even the creator of Philo Vance, only make the Junior Varsity.

This, the classic detective story, has learned nothing and forgotten nothing. It is the story you will find almost any week in the big shiny magazines, handsomely illustrated, and paying due deference to virginal love and the right kind of luxury goods. Perhaps the tempo has become a trifle faster and the dialogue a little more glib. There are more frozen daiquiris and stingers and fewer glasses of crusty old port, more clothes by *Vogue* and décors by *House Beautiful,* more chic, but not more truth. We spend more time in Miami hotels and Cape Cod summer colonies and go not so often down by the old gray sundial in the Elizabethan garden.

But fundamentally it is the same careful grouping of suspects, the same utterly incomprehensible trick of how somebody stabbed Mrs. Pottington Postlethwaite

III with the solid platinum poniard just as she flatted on the top note of the "Bell Song" from *Lakmé* in the presence of fifteen ill-assorted guests; the same ingénue in fur-trimmed pajamas screaming in the night to make the company pop in and out of doors and ball up the timetable; the same moody silence next day as they sit around sipping Singapore slings and sneering at each other, while the flatfeet crawl to and fro under the Persian rugs, with their derby hats on.

Personally I like the English style better. It is not quite so brittle and the people as a rule just wear clothes and drink drinks. There is more sense of background, as if Cheesecake Manor really existed all around and not just in the part the camera sees; there are more long walks over the downs and the characters don't all try to behave as if they had just been tested by MGM. The English may not always be the best writers in the world, but they are incomparably the best dull writers.

There is a very simple statement to be made about all these stories: they do not really come off intellectually as problems, and they do not come off artistically as fiction. They are too contrived, and too little aware of what goes on in the world. They try to be honest, but honesty is an art. The poor writer is dishonest without knowing it, and the fairly good one can be dishonest because he doesn't know what to be honest about. He thinks a complicated murder scheme which baffled the lazy reader, who won't be bothered itemizing the details, will also baffle the police, whose business is with details.

The boys with their feet on the desks know that the easiest murder case in the world to break is the one somebody tried to get very cute with; the one that really bothers them is the murder somebody thought of only two minutes before he pulled it off. But if the writers of this fiction wrote about the kind of murders that happen, they would also have to write about the authentic flavor of life as it is lived. And since they cannot do that, they pretend that what they do is what should be done. Which is begging the question—and the best of them know it.

In her introduction to the first *Omnibus of Crime,* Dorothy Sayers wrote: "It [the detective story] does not, and by hypothesis never can, attain the loftiest level of literary achievement." And she suggested somewhere else that this is because it is a "literature of escape" and not "a literature of expression." I do not know what the loftiest level of literary achievement is: neither did Aeschylus or Shakespeare; neither does Miss Sayers. Other things being equal, which they never are, a more powerful theme will provoke a more powerful performance. Yet some very dull books have been written about God, and some very fine ones about how to make a living and stay fairly honest. It is always a matter of who writes the stuff, and what he has in him to write it with.

As for "literature of expression" and "literature of escape"—this is critics' jargon, a use of abstract words as if they had absolute meanings. Everything written with vitality expresses that vitality: there are no dull subjects, only dull minds. All men who read escape from something else into what lies behind the printed page; the quality of the dream may be argued, but its release has become a functional necessity. All men must escape at times from the deadly rhythm of their private thoughts. It is part of the process of life among thinking beings. It is one of the things that distinguish them from the three-toed sloth; he apparently—one can never be quite sure—is perfectly content hanging upside down on a branch, not even reading Walter

Lippmann. I hold no particular brief for the detective story as the ideal escape. I merely say that *all* reading for pleasure is escape, whether it be Greek, mathematics, astronomy, Benedetto Croce, or The Diary of the Forgotten Man. To say otherwise is to be an intellectual snob, and a juvenile at the art of living.

I do not think such considerations moved Miss Dorothy Sayers to her essay in critical futility.

I think what was really gnawing at Miss Sayers' mind was the slow realization that her kind of detective story was an arid formula which could not even satisfy its own implications. It was second-grade literature because it was not about the things that could make first-grade literature. If it started out to be about real people (and she could write about them—her minor characters show that), they must very soon do unreal things in order to form the artificial pattern required by the plot. When they did unreal things, they ceased to be real themselves. They became puppets and cardboard lovers and papier-mâché villains and detectives of exquisite and impossible gentility.

The only kind of writer who could be happy with these properties was the one who did not know what reality was. Dorothy Sayers' own stories show that she was annoyed by this triteness; the weakest element in them is the part that makes them detective stories, the strongest the part which could be removed without touching the "problem of logic and deduction." Yet she could not or would not give her characters their heads and let them make their own mystery. It took a much simpler and more direct mind than hers to do that.

In *The Long Week End,* which is a drastically competent account of English life and manners in the decades following the First World War, Robert Graves and Alan Hodge gave some attention to the detective story.

They were just as traditionally English as the ornaments of the Golden Age, and they wrote of the time in which these writers were almost as well known as any writers in the world. Their books in one form or another sold into the millions, and in a dozen languages. These were the people who fixed the form and established the rules and founded the famous Detection Club, which is a Parnassus of English writers of mystery. Its roster includes practically every important writer of detective fiction since Conan Doyle.

But Graves and Hodge decided that during this whole period only one first-class writer had written detective stories at all. An American, Dashiell Hammett. Traditional or not, Graves and Hodge were not fuddy-duddy connoisseurs of the second-rate; they could see what went on in the world and that the detective story of their time didn't; and they were aware that writers who have the vision and the ability to produce real fiction do not produce unreal fiction.

How original a writer Hammett really was it isn't easy to decide now, even if it mattered. He was one of a group—the only one who achieved critical recognition—who wrote or tried to write realistic mystery fiction. All literary movements are like this; some one individual is picked out to represent the whole movement; he is usually the culmination of the movement. Hammett was the ace performer, but there is nothing in his work that is not implicit in the early novels and short stories of Hemingway.

Yet, for all I know, Hemingway, may have learned something from Hammett as well as from writers like Dreiser, Ring Lardner, Carl Sandburg, Sherwood Anderson, and himself. A rather revolutionary debunking of both the language and the material of fiction had been going on for some time. It probably started in poetry; almost everything does. You can take it clear back to Walt Whitman, if you like. But Hammett applied it to the detective story, and this, because of its heavy crust of English gentility and American pseudo-gentility, was pretty hard to get moving.

I doubt that Hammett had any deliberate artistic aims whatever; he was trying to make a living by writing something he had firsthand information about. He made some of it up; all writers do; but it had a basis in fact; it was made up out of real things. The only reality the English detection writers knew was the conversational accent of Surbiton and Bognor Regis. If they wrote about dukes and Venetian vases, they knew no more about them out of their own experience than the well-heeled Hollywood character knows about the French Modernists that hang in his Bel-Air château or the semi-antique Chippendale-cum-cobbler's bench that he uses for a coffee table. Hammett took murder out of the Venetian vase and dropped it into the alley; it doesn't have to stay there forever, but it looked like a good idea to get as far as possible from Emily Post's idea of how a well-bred débutante gnaws a chicken wing.

Hammett wrote at first (and almost to the end) for people with a sharp, aggressive attitude to life. They were not afraid of the seamy side of things; they lived there. Violence did not dismay them; it was right down their street. Hammett gave murder back to the kind of people that commit it for reasons, not just to provide a corpse; and with the means at hand, not hand-wrought dueling pistols, curare and tropical fish. He put these people down on paper as they were, and he made them talk and think in the language they customarily used for these purposes.

He had style, but his audience didn't know it, because it was in a language not supposed to be capable of such refinements. They thought they were getting a good meaty melodrama written in the kind of lingo they imagined they spoke themselves. It was, in a sense, but it was much more. All language begins with speech, and the speech of common men at that, but when it develops to the point of becoming a literary medium it only looks like speech. Hammett's style at its worst was as formalized as a page of *Marius the Epicurean;* at its best it could say almost anything. I believe this style, which does not belong to Hammett or to anybody, but is the American language (and not even exclusively that any more), can say things he did not know how to say, or feel the need of saying. In his hands it had no overtones, left no echo, evoked no image beyond a distant hill.

Hammett is said to have lacked heart; yet the story he himself thought the most of is the record of a man's devotion to a friend. He was spare, frugal, hard-boiled, but he did over and over again what only the best writers can ever do at all. He wrote scenes that seemed never to have been written before.

With all this he did not wreck the formal detective story. Nobody can; production demands a form that can be produced. Realism takes too much talent, too much knowledge, too much awareness. Hammett may have loosened it up a little here, and sharpened it a little there. Certainly all but the stupidest and most meretricious writers are more conscious of their artificiality than they used to be. And he demonstrated that the detective story can be important writing. *The Maltese Falcon* may or may not be a work of genius, but an art which is capable of it is not "by hypothesis" incapable of anything. Once a detective story can be as good as this, only the pedants will deny that it *could* be even better.

Hammett did something else; he made the detective

story fun to write, not an exhausting concatenation of insignificant clues. Without him there might not have been a regional mystery as clever as Percival Wilde's *Inquest,* or an ironic study as able as Raymond Postgate's *Verdict of Twelve,* or a savage piece of intellectual double-talk like Kenneth Fearing's *The Dagger of the Mind,* or a tragi-comic idealization of the murderer as in Donald Henderson's *Mr. Bowling Buys a Newspaper,* or even a gay Hollywoodian gambol like Richard Sale's *Lazarus No. 7.*

The realistic style is easy to abuse: from haste, from lack of awareness, from inability to bridge the chasm that lies between what a writer would like to be able to say and what he actually knows how to say. It is easy to fake; brutality is not strength, flipness is not wit, edge-of-the-chair writing can be as boring as flat writing; dalliance with promiscuous blondes can be very dull stuff when described by goaty young men with no other purpose in mind than to describe dalliance with promiscuous blondes. There has been so much of this sort of thing that if a character in a detective story says "Yeah," the author is automatically a Hammett imitator.

And there are still a number of people around who say that Hammett did not write detective stories at all—merely hard-boiled chronicles of mean streets with a perfunctory mystery element dropped in like the olive in a martini. These are the flustered old ladies—of both sexes (or no sex) and almost all ages—who like their murders scented with magnolia blossoms and do not care to be reminded that murder is an act of infinite cruelty, even if the perpetrators sometimes look like playboys or college professors or nice motherly women with softly graying hair.

There are also a few badly scared champions of the formal or classic mystery who think that no story is a detective story which does not pose a formal and exact problem and arrange the clues around it with neat labels on them. Such would point out, for example, that in reading *The Maltese Falcon* no one concerns himself with who killed Spade's partner, Archer (which is the only formal problem of the story), because the reader is kept thinking about something else. Yet in *The Glass Key* the reader is constantly reminded that the question is who killed Taylor Henry, and exactly the same effect is obtained—an effect of movement, intrigue, cross-purposes, and the gradual elucidation of character, which is all the detective story has any right to be about anyway. The rest is spillikins in the parlor.

But all this (and Hammett too) is for me not quite enough. The realist in murder writes of a world in which gangsters can rule nations and almost rule cities, in which hotels and apartment houses and celebrated restaurants are owned by men who made their money out of brothels, in which a screen star can be the finger man for a mob, and the nice man down the hall is a boss of the numbers racket; a world where a judge with a cellar full of bootleg liquor can send a man to jail for having a pint in his pocket, where the mayor of your town may have condoned murder as an instrument of money-making, where no man can walk down a dark street in safety because law and order are things we talk about but refrain from practicing; a world where you may witness a holdup in broad daylight and see who did it, but you will fade quickly back into the crowd rather than tell anyone, because the holdup men may have friends with long guns, or the police may not like your testimony, and in any case the shyster for the defense will be allowed to abuse and vilify you in open court, before a jury of selected morons, without any but the most perfunctory interference from a political judge.

It is not a fragrant world, but it is the world you live in, and certain writers with tough minds and a cool spirit of detachment can make very interesting and even amusing patterns out of it. It is not funny that a man should be killed, but it is sometimes funny that he should be killed for so little, and that his death should be the coin of what we call civilization. All this still is not quite enough.

In everything that can be called art there is a quality of redemption. It may be pure tragedy, if it is high tragedy, and it may be pity and irony, and it may be the raucous laughter of the strong man. But down these mean streets a man must go who is not himself mean, who is neither tarnished nor afraid. The detective in this kind of story must be such a man. He is the hero; he is everything. He must be a complete man and a common man and yet an unusual man. He must be, to use a rather weathered phrase, a man of honor—by instinct, by inevitability, without thought of it, and certainly without saying it. He must be the best man in his world and a good enough man for any world. I do not care much about his private life; he is neither a eunuch nor a satyr; I think he might seduce a duchess and I am quite sure he would not spoil a virgin; if he is a man of honor in one thing, he is that in all things.

He is a relatively poor man, or he would not be a detective at all. He is a common man or he could not go among common people. He has a sense of character, or he would not know his job. He will take no man's money dishonestly and no man's insolence without a due and dispassionate revenge. He is a lonely man and his pride is that you will treat him as a proud man or be very sorry you ever saw him. He talks as the man of his age talks—that is, with rude wit, a lively sense of the grotesque, a disgust for sham, and a contempt for pettiness.

The story is this man's adventure in search of a hidden truth, and it would be no adventure if it did not happen to a man fit for adventure. He has a range of awareness that startles you, but it belongs to him by right, because it belongs to the world he lives in. If there were enough like him, the world would be a very safe place to live in, without becoming too dull to be worth living in.

# SPANISH BLOOD

Big John Masters was large, fat, oily. He had sleek blue jowls and very thick fingers on which the knuckles were dimples. His brown hair was combed straight back from his forehead and he wore a wine-colored suit with patch pockets, a wine-colored tie, a tan silk shirt. There was a lot of red and gold band around the thick brown cigar between his lips.

He wrinkled his nose, peeped at his hole card again, tried not to grin. He said: "Hit me again, Dave—and don't hit me with the City Hall."

A four and a deuce showed. Dave Aage looked at them solemnly across the table, looked down at his own hand. He was very tall and thin, with a long bony face and hair the color of wet sand. He held the deck flat on the palm of his hand, turned the top card slowly, and flicked it across the table. It was the queen of spades.

Big John Masters opened his mouth wide, waved his cigar about, chuckled.

"Pay me, Dave. For once a lady was right." He turned his hole card with a flourish. A five.

Dave Aage smiled politely, didn't move. A muted telephone bell rang close to him, behind long silk drapes that bordered the very high lancet windows. He took a cigarette out of his mouth and laid it carefully on the edge of a tray on a tabouret beside the card table, reached behind the curtain for the phone.

He spoke into the cup with a cool, almost whispering voice, then listened for a long time. Nothing changed in his greenish eyes, no flicker of emotion showed on his narrow face. Masters squirmed, bit hard on his cigar.

After a long time Aage said, "Okey, you'll hear from us." He pronged the instrument and put it back behind the curtain.

He picked his cigarette up, pulled the lobe of hs ear. Masters swore. "What's eating you, for Pete's sake? Gimme ten bucks."

Aage smiled dryly and leaned back. He reached for a drink, sipped it, put it down, spoke around his cigarette. All his movements were slow, thoughtful, almost absent-minded. He said: "Are we a couple of smart guys, John?"

"Yeah. We own the town. But it don't help my blackjack game any."

"It's just two months to election, isn't it, John?"

Masters scowled at him, fished in his pocket for a fresh cigar, jammed it into his mouth.

"So what?"

"Suppose something happened to our toughest opposition. Right now. Would that be a good idea, or not?"

"Huh?" Masters raised eyebrows so thick that his whole face seemed to have to work to push them up.

He thought for a moment, sourly. "It would be lousy—
if they didn't catch the guy pronto. Hell, the voters
would figure we hired it done."

"You're talking about murder, John," Aage said
patiently. "I didn't say anything about murder."

Masters lowered his eyebrows and pulled at a coarse
black hair that grew out of his nose.

"Well, spit it out!"

Aage smiled, blew a smoke ring, watched it float off
and come apart in frail wisps.

"I just had a phone call," he said very softly. "Donegan Marr is dead."

Masters moved slowly. His whole body moved slowly towards the card table, leaned far over it. When his
body couldn't go any farther his chin came out until his
jaw muscles stood out like thick wires.

"Huh?" he said thickly. "Huh?"

Aage nodded, calm as ice. "But you were right about
murder, John. It *was* murder. Just half an hour ago, or
so. In his office. They don't know who did it—yet."

Masters shrugged heavily and leaned back. He
looked around him with a stupid expression. Very suddenly he began to laugh. His laughter bellowed and
roared around the little turretlike room where the two
men sat, overflowed into an enormous living room beyond, echoed back and forth through a maze of heavy
dark furniture, enough standing lamps to light a boulevard, a double row of oil paintings in massive gold
frames.

Aage sat silent. He rubbed his cigarette out slowly in
the tray until there was nothing of the fire left but a
thick dark smudge. He dusted his bony fingers together and waited.

Masters stopped laughing as abruptly as he had be-
gun. The room was very still. Masters looked tired. He
mopped his big face.

"We got to do something, Dave," he said quietly. "I almost forgot. We got to break this fast. It's dynamite."

Aage reached behind the curtain again and brought the phone out, pushed it across the table over the scattered cards.

"Well—we know how, don't we?" he said calmly.

A cunning light shone in Big John Masters' muddy brown eyes. He licked his lips, reached a big hand for the phone.

"Yeah," he said purringly, "we do, Dave. We do at that, by——!"

He dialed with a thick finger that would hardly go into the holes.

## 2

Donegan Marr's face looked cool, neat, poised, even then. He was dressed in soft gray flannels and his hair was the same soft gray color as his suit, brushed back from a ruddy, youngish face. The skin was pale on the frontal bones where the hair would fall when he stood up. The rest of the skin was tanned.

He was lying back in a padded blue office chair. A cigar had gone out in a tray with a bronze greyhound on its rim. His left hand dangled beside the chair and his right hand held a gun loosely on the desk top. The polished nails glittered in sunlight from the big closed window behind him.

Blood had soaked the left side of his vest, made the gray flannel almost black. He was quite dead, had been dead for some time.

A tall man, very brown and slender and silent, leaned against a brown mahogany filing cabinet and looked fixedly at the dead man. His hands were in the pockets of a neat blue serge suit. There was a straw hat

on the back of his head. But there was nothing casual
about his eyes or his tight, straight mouth.

A big sandy-haired man was groping around on the
blue rug. He said thickly, stooped over: "No shells,
Sam."

The dark man didn't move, didn't answer. The other
stood up, yawned, looked at the man in the chair.

"Hell! This one will stink. Two months to election.
Boy, is this a smack in the puss for somebody."

The dark man said slowly: "We went to school together. We used to be buddies. We carried the torch
for the same girl. He won, but we stayed good friends,
all three of us. He was always a great kid . . . Maybe a
shade too smart."

The sandy-haired man walked around the room
without touching anything. He bent over and sniffed at
the gun on the desk, shook his head, said: "Not used—
this one." He wrinkled his nose, sniffed at the air. "Air-
conditioned. The three top floors. Soundproofed too.
High-grade stuff. They tell me this whole building is
electric-welded. Not a rivet in it. Ever hear that, Sam?"

The dark man shook his head slowly.

"Wonder where the help was," the sandy-haired
man went on. "A big shot like him would have more
than one girl."

The dark man shook his head again. "That's all, I
guess. She was out to lunch. He was a lone wolf, Pete.
Sharp as a weasel. In a few more years he'd have taken
the town over."

The sandy-haired man was behind the desk now, almost leaning over the dead man's shoulder. He was
looking down at a leather-backed appointment pad
with buff leaves. He said slowly: "Somebody named
Imlay was due here at twelve-fifteen. Only date on the
pad."

He glanced at a cheap watch on his wrist. "One-thirty. Long gone. Who's Imlay? . . . Say, wait a minute! There's an assistant D.A. named Imlay. He's running for judge on the Master-Aage ticket. D'you figure——"

There was a sharp knock on the door. The office was so long that the two men had to think a moment before they placed which of the three doors it was. Then the sandy-haired man went towards the most distant of them, saying over his shoulder: "M.E's man maybe. Leak this to your favorite newshawk and you're out a job. Am I right?"

The dark man didn't answer. He moved slowly to the desk, leaned forward a little, spoke softly to the dead man.

"Goodbye, Donny. Just let it all go. I'll take care of it. I'll take care of Belle."

The door at the end of the office opened and a brisk man with a bag came in, trotted down the blue carpet and put his bag on the desk. The sandy-haired man shut the door against a bulge of faces. He strolled back to the desk.

The brisk man cocked his head on one side, examining the corpse. "Two of them," he muttered. "Look like about .32's—hard slugs. Close to the heart but not touching. He must have died pretty soon. Maybe a minute or two."

The dark man made a disgusted sound and walked to the window, stood with his back to the room, looking out, at the tops of high buildings and a warm blue sky. The sandy-haired man watched the examiner lift a dead eyelid. He said: "Wish the powder guy would get here. I wanta use the phone. This Imlay——"

The dark man turned his head slightly, with a dull smile. "Use it. This isn't going to be any mystery."

"Oh I don't know," the M.E.'s man said, flexing a wrist, then holding the back of his hand against the skin of the dead man's face. "Might not be so damn political as you think, Delaguerra. He's a good-looking stiff."

The sandy-haired man took hold of the phone gingerly, with a handkerchief, laid the receiver down, dialed, picked the receiver up with the handkerchief and put it to his ear.

After a moment he snapped his chin down, said: "Pete Marcus. Wake the Inspector." He yawned, waited again, then spoke in a different tone: "Marcus and Delaguerra, Inspector, from Donegan Marr's office. No print or camera men here yet . . . Huh? . . . Holding off till the Commissioner gets here? . . . Okey . . . Yeah, he's here."

The dark man turned. The man at the phone gestured at him. "Take it, Spanish."

Sam Delaguerra took the phone, ignoring the careful handkerchief, listened. His face got hard. He said quietly: "Sure I knew him—but I didn't sleep with him . . . Nobody's here but his secretary, a girl. She phoned the alarm in. There's a name on a pad—Imlay, a twelve-fifteen appointment. No, we haven't touched anything yet . . . No . . . Okey, right away."

He hung up so slowly that the click of the instrument was barely audible. His hand stayed on it, then fell suddenly and heavily to his side. His voice was thick.

"I'm called off it, Pete. You're to hold it down until Commissioner Drew gets here. Nobody gets in. White, black or Cherokee Indian."

"What you called in for?" the sandy-haired man yelped angrily.

"Don't know. It's an order," Delaguerra said tonelessly.

The M.E.'s man stopped writing on a form pad to look curiously at Delaguerra, with a sharp, sidelong look.

Delaguerra crossed the office and went through the

communicating door. There was a smaller office outside, partly partitioned off for a waiting room, with a
group of leather chairs and a table with magazines. Inside a counter was a typewriter desk, a safe, some filing
cabinets. A small dark girl sat at the desk with her head
down on a wadded handkerchief. Her hat was crooked
on her head. Her shoulders jerked and her thick sobs
were like panting.

Delaguerra patted her shoulder. She looked up at
him with a tear-bloated face, a twisted mouth. He
smiled down at her questioning face, said gently: "Did
you call Mrs. Marr yet?"

She nodded, speechless, shaken with rough sobs. He
patted her shoulder again, stood a moment beside her,
then went on out, with his mouth tight and a hard, dark
glitter in his black eyes.

## 3

The big English house stood a long way back from the
narrow, winding ribbon of concrete that was called De
Neve Lane. The lawn had rather long grass with a
curving path of stepping stones half hidden in it. There
was a gable over the front door and ivy on the wall.
Trees grew all around the house, close to it, made it a
little dark and remote.

All the houses in De Neve Lane had that same cal-
culated air of neglect. But the tall green hedge that hid
the driveway and the garages was trimmed as carefully
as a French poodle, and there was nothing dark or mys-
terious about the mass of yellow and flame-colored
gladioli that flared at the opposite end of the lawn.

Delaguerra got out of a tan-colored Cadillac tour-
ing car that had no top. It was an old model, heavy
and dirty. A taut canvas formed a deck over the back
part of the car. He wore a white linen cap and dark

glasses and had changed his blue serge for a gray cloth outing suit with a jerkin-style zipper jacket.

He didn't look very much like a cop. He hadn't looked very much like a cop in Donegan Marr's office. He walked slowly up the path of stepping stones, touched a brass knocker on the front door of the house, then didn't knock with it. He pushed a bell at the side, almost hidden by the ivy.

There was a long wait. It was very warm, very silent. Bees droned over the warm bright grass. There was the distant whirring of a lawnmower.

The door opened slowly and a black face looked out at him, a long, sad black face with tear streaks on its lavender face powder. The black face almost smiled, said haltingly: "Hello there, Mistah Sam. It's sure good to see you."

Delaguerra took his cap off, swung the dark glasses at his side. He said: "Hello, Minnie. I'm sorry. I've got to see Mrs. Marr."

"Sure. Come right in, Mistah Sam."

The maid stood aside and he went into a shadowy hall with a tile floor. "No reporters yet?"

The girl shook her head slowly. Her warm brown eyes were stunned, doped with shock.

"Ain't been nobody yet . . . She ain't been in long. She ain't said a word. She just stand there in that there sun room that ain't got no sun."

Delaguerra nodded, said: "Don't talk to anybody, Minnie. They're trying to keep this quiet for a while, out of the papers."

"Ah sure won't, Mistah Sam. Not nohow."

Delaguerra smiled at her, walked noiselessly on crêpe soles along the tiled hall to the back of the house, turned into another hall just like it at right angles. He knocked at a door. There was no answer. He turned the knob and went into a long narrow room that was dim in spite of many windows. Trees grew close to the windows, pressing their leaves against the glass. Some of the windows were masked by long cretonne drapes.

The tall girl in the middle of the room didn't look at him. She stood motionless, rigid. She stared at the windows. Her hands were tightly clenched at her sides.

She had red-brown hair that seemed to gather all the light there was and make a soft halo around her coldly beautiful face. She wore a sportily cut blue velvet ensemble with patch pockets. A white handkerchief with a blue border stuck out of the breast pocket, arranged carefully in points, like a foppish man's handkerchief.

Delaguerra waited, letting his eyes get used to the dimness. After a while the girl spoke through the silence, in a low, husky voice.

"Well . . . they got him, Sam. They got him at last. Was he so much hated?"

Delaguerra said softly: "He was in a tough racket, Belle. I guess he played it as clean as he could, but he couldn't help but make enemies."

She turned her head slowly and looked at him. Lights shifted in her hair. Gold glinted in it. Her eyes were vividly, startlingly blue. Her voice faltered a little, saying: "Who killed him, Sam? Have they any ideas?"

Delaguerra nodded slowly, sat down in a wicker chair, swung his cap and glasses between his knees.

"Yeah. We think we know who did it. A man named Imlay, an assistant in the D.A.'s office."

"My God!" the girl breathed. "What's this rotten city coming to?"

Delaguerra went on tonelessly: "It was like this—if you're sure you want to know . . . yet."

"I do, Sam. His eyes stare at me from the wall, wherever I look. Asking me to do something. He was pretty swell to me, Sam. We had our troubles, of course, but . . . they didn't mean anything."

Delaguerra said: "This Imlay is running for judge with the backing of the Masters-Aage group. He's in and the gay forties and it seems he's been playing house with a night-club number called Stella La Motte. Somehow, someway, photos were taken of them together, very drunk and undressed. Donny got the photos, Belle. They were found in his desk. According to his desk pad he had a date with Imlay at twelve-fifteen. We figure they had a row and Imlay beat him to the punch."

"You found those photos, Sam?" the girl asked, very quietly.

He shook his head, smiled crookedly. "No. If I had, I guess I might have ditched them. Commissioner Drew found them—after I was pulled off the investigation."

Her head jerked at him. Her vivid blue eyes got wide. "Pulled off the investigation? You—Donny's friend?"

"Yeah. Don't take it too big. I'm a cop, Belle. After all I take orders."

She didn't speak, didn't look at him any more. After a little while he said: "I'd like to have the keys to your cabin at Puma Lake. I'm detailed to go up there and look around, see if there's any evidence. Donny had conferences there."

Something changed in the girl's face. It got almost contemptuous. Her voice was empty. "I'll get them. But you won't find anything there. If you're helping them to find dirt on Donny—so they can clear this Imlay person. . . ."

He smiled a little, shook his head slowly. His eyes were very deep, very sad.

"That's crazy talk, kid. I'd turn my badge in before I did that."

"I see." She walked past him to the door, went out of the room. He sat quite still while she was gone, looked at the wall with an empty stare. There was a hurt look on his face. He swore very softly, under his breath.

The girl came back, walked up to him and held her hand out. Something tinkled into his palm.

"The keys, copper."

Delaguerra stood up, dropped the keys into a pocket. His face got wooden. Belle Marr went over to a table and her nails scratched harshly on a cloisonné box, getting a cigarette out of it. With her back turned she said: "I don't think you'll have any luck, as I said. It's too bad you've only got blackmailing on him so far."

Delaguerra breathed out slowly, stood a moment, then turned away. "Okey," he said softly. His voice was quite offhand now, as if it was a nice day, as if nobody had been killed.

At the door he turned again. "I'll see you when I get back, Belle. Maybe you'll feel better."

She didn't answer, didn't move. She held the unlighted cigarette rigidly in front of her mouth, close to it. After a moment Delaguerra went on: "You ought to know how I feel about it. Donny and I were like brothers once. I——I heard you were not getting on so well with him . . . I'm glad as all hell that was wrong. But don't let yourself get too hard, Belle. There's nothing to be hard about—with me."

He waited a few seconds, staring at her back. When she still didn't move or speak he went on out.

# 4

A narrow rocky road dropped down from the highway and ran along the flank of the hill above the lake. The tops of cabins showed here and there among the pines. An open shed was cut into the side of the hill. Delaguerra put his dusty Cadillac under it and climbed down a narrow path towards the water.

The lake was deep blue but very low. Two or three canoes drifted about on it and the chugging of an outboard motor sounded in the distance, around a bend. He went along between thick walls of undergrowth, walking on pine needles, turned around a stump and crossed a small rustic bridge to the Marr cabin.

It was built of half-round logs and had a wide porch on the lake side. It looked very lonely and empty. The spring that ran under the bridge curved around beside the house and one end of the porch dropped down sheer to the big flat stones through which the water trickled. The stones would be covered when the water was high, in the spring.

Delaguerra went up wooden steps and took the keys out of his pocket, unlocked the heavy front door, then stood on the porch a little while and lit a cigarette before he went in. It was very still, very pleasant, very cool and clear after the heat of the city. A mountain bluejay sat on a stump and pecked at its wings. Somebody far out on the lake fooled with a ukulele. He went into the cabin.

He looked at some dusty antlers, a big rough table splattered with magazines, an old-fashioned battery-type radio, a box-shaped phonograph with a disheveled pile of records beside it. There were tall glasses that hadn't been washed and a half-bottle of Scotch beside them, on a table near the big stone fireplace. A car went along the road up above and stopped somewhere not far off. Delaguerra frowned around, said: "Stall," under his breath, with a defeated feeling. There wasn't any sense in it. A man like Donegan Marr wouldn't leave anything that mattered in a mountain cabin.

He looked into a couple of bedrooms, one just a shake-down with a couple of cots, one better furnished, with a make-up bed, and a pair of women's gaudy pajamas tossed across it. They didn't look quite like Belle Marr's.

At the back there was a small kitchen with a gasoline stove and a wood stove. He opened the back door with another key and stepped out on a small porch flush with the ground, near a big pile of cordwood and a double-bitted axe on a chopping block.

Then he saw the flies.

A wooden walk went down the side of the house to a woodshed under it. A beam of sunlight had slipped through the trees and lay across the walk. In the sunlight there a clotted mass of flies festered on something brownish, sticky. The flies didn't want to move. Delaguerra bent down, then put his hand down and touched the sticky place, sniffed at his finger. His face got shocked and stiff.

There was another smaller patch of the brownish stuff farther on, in the shade, outside the door of the shed. He took the keys out of his pocket very quickly and found the one that unlocked the big padlock of the woodshed. He yanked the door open.

There was a big loose pile of cordwood inside. Not split wood—cordwood. Not stacked, just thrown in anyhow. Delaguerra began to toss the big rough pieces to one side.

After he had thrown a lot of it aside he was able to reach down and take hold of two cold stiff ankles in lisle socks and drag the dead man out into the light.

He was a slender man, neither tall nor short, in a well-cut basket weave suit. His small neat shoes were polished, a little dust over the polish. He didn't have any face, much. It was broken to pulp by a terrific smash. The top of his head was split open and brains and blood were mixed in the thin grayish-brown hair.

Delaguerra straightened quickly and went back into the house to where the half-bottle of Scotch stood on the table in the living room. He uncorked it, drank from the neck, waited a moment, drank again.

He said: "Phew!" out loud, and shivered as the whiskey whipped at his nerves.

He went back to the woodshed, leaned down again as an automobile motor started up somewhere. He stiffened. The motor swelled in sound, then the sound faded and there was silence again. Delaguerra shrugged, went through the dead man's pockets. They were empty. One of them, with cleaner's marks on it probably, had been cut away. The tailor's label had been cut from the inside pocket of the coat, leaving ragged stitches.

The man was stiff. He might have been dead twenty-four hours, not more. The blood on his face had coagulated thickly but had not dried completely.

Delaguerra squatted beside him for a little while, looking at the bright glitter of Puma Lake, the distant flash of a paddle from a canoe. Then he went back into the woodshed and pawed around for a heavy block of wood with a great deal of blood on it, didn't find one. He went back into the house and out on the front porch, went to the end of the porch, stared down the drop, then at the big flat stones in the spring.

"Yeah," he said softly.

There were flies clotted on two of the stones, a lot of flies. He hadn't noticed them before. The drop was about thirty feet, enough to smash a man's head open if he landed just right.

He sat down in one of the big rockers and smoked for several minutes without moving. His face was still with thought, his black eyes withdrawn and remote. There was a tight, hard smile, ever so faintly sardonic, at the corners of his mouth.

At the end of that he went silently back through the house and dragged the dead man into the woodshed again, covered him up loosely with the wood. He locked the woodshed, locked the house up, went back along the narrow, steep path to the road and to his car.

It was past six o'clock, but the sun was still bright as he drove off.

## 5

An old store counter served as bar in the roadside beer-stube. Three low stools stood against it. Delaguerra sat on the end one near the door, looked at the foamy inside of an empty beer glass. The bartender was a dark kid in overalls, with shy eyes and lank hair. He stuttered. He said: "Sh-should I d-draw you another g-glass, mister?"

Delaguerra shook his head, stood up off the stool. "Racket beer, sonny," he said sadly. "Tasteless as a roadhouse blonde."

"P-portola B-brew, mister. Supposed to be the b-best."

"Uh-huh. The worst. You use it, or you don't have a license. So long, sonny."

He went across to the screen door, looked out at the sunny highway on which the shadows were getting quite long. Beyond the concrete there was a graveled space edged by a white fence of four-by-fours. There were two cars parked there: Delaguerra's old Cadillac and a dusty hard-bitten Ford. A tall, thin man in khaki whipcord stood beside the Cadillac, looking at it.

Delaguerra got a bulldog pipe out, filled it half full from a zipper pouch, lit it with slow care and flicked the match into the corner. Then he stiffened a little, looking out through the screen.

The tall, thin man was unsnapping the canvas that covered the back part of Delaguerra's car. He rolled part of it back, stood peering down in the space underneath.

Delaguerra opened the screen door softly and walked in long, loose strides across the concrete of the highway. His crêpe soles made sound on the gravel beyond, but the thin man didn't turn. Delaguerra came up beside him.

"Thought I noticed you behind me," he said dully. "What's the grift?"

The man turned without any haste. He had a long, sour face, eyes the color of seaweed. His coat was open, pushed back by a hand on a left hip. That showed a gun worn butt to the front in a belt holster, cavalry style.

He looked Delaguerra up and down with a faint crooked smile.

"This your crate?"

"What do you think?"

The thin man pulled his coat back farther and showed a bronze badge on his pocket.

"I think I'm a Toluca County game warden, mister. I think this ain't deer-hunting time and it ain't ever deer-hunting time for does."

Delaguerra lowered his eyes very slowly, looked into the back of his car, bending over to see past the canvas. The body of a young deer lay there on some junk, beside a rifle. The soft eyes of the dead animal, unglazed by death, seemed to look at him with a gentle reproach. There was dried blood on the doe's slender neck.

Delaguerra straightened, said gently: "That's damn cute."

"Got a hunting license?"

"I don't hunt," Delaguerra said.

"Wouldn't help much. I see you got a rifle."

"I'm a cop."

"Oh—cop, huh? Would you have a badge?"

"I would."

Delaguerra reached into his breast pocket, got the badge out, rubbed it on his sleeve, held it in the palm of his hand. The thin game warden stared down at it, licking his lips.

"Detective lieutenant, huh? City police." His face got distant and lazy. "Okey, Lieutenant. We'll ride about ten miles downgrade in your heap. I'll thumb a ride back to mine."

Delaguerra put the badge away, knocked his pipe out carefully, stamped the embers into the gravel. He replaced the canvas loosely.

"Pinched?" he asked gravely.

"Pinched, Lieutenant."

"Let's go."

He got in under the wheel of the Cadillac. The thin warden went around the other side, got in beside him. Delaguerra started the car, backed around and started off down the smooth concrete of the highway. The valley was a deep haze in the distance. Beyond the haze other peaks were enormous on the skyline. Delaguerra coasted the big car easily, without haste. The two men stared straight before them without speaking.

After a long time Delaguerra said: "I didn't know they had deer at Puma Lake. That's as far as I've been."

"There's a reservation by there, Lieutenant," the

warden said calmly. He stared through the dusty windshield. "Part of the Toluca County Forest—or wouldn't you know that?"

Delaguerra said: "I guess I wouldn't know it. I never shot a deer in my life. Police work hasn't made me that tough."

The warden grinned, said nothing. The highway went through a saddle, then the drop was on the right side of the highway. Little canyons began to open out into the hills on the left. Some of them had rough roads in them, half overgrown, with wheel tracks.

Delaguerra swung the big car hard and suddenly to the left, shot it into a cleared space of reddish earth and dry grass, slammed the brake on. The car skidded, swayed, ground to a lurching stop.

The warden was flung violently to the right, then forward against the windshield. He cursed, jerked up straight and threw his right hand across his body at the holstered gun.

Delaguerra took hold of a thin, hard wrist and twisted it sharply towards the man's body. The warden's face whitened behind the tan. His left hand fumbled at the holster, then relaxed. He spoke in a tight, hurt voice.

"Makin' it worse, copper. I got a phone tip at Salt Springs. Described your car, said where it was. Said there was a doe carcass in it. I—"

Delaguerra loosed the wrist, snapped the belt holster open and jerked the Colt out of it. He tossed the gun from the car.

"Get out, County! Thumb that ride you spoke of. What's the matter—can't you live on your salary any more? You planted it yourself, back at Puma Lake, you goddamn chiseler!"

The warden got out slowly, stood on the ground with his face blank, his jaw loose and slack.

"Tough guy," he muttered. "You'll be sorry for this, copper. I'll swear a complaint."

Delaguerra slid across the seat, got out of the right-hand door. He stood close to the warden, said very slowly: "Maybe I'm wrong, mister. Maybe you did get a call. Maybe you did."

He swung the doe's body out of the car, laid it down on the ground, watching the warden. The thin man didn't move, didn't try to get near his gun lying on the grass a dozen feet away. His seaweed eyes were dull, very cold.

Delaguerra got back into the Cadillac, snapped the brake off, started the engine. He backed to the highway. The warden still didn't make a move.

The Cadillac leaped forward, shot down the grade, out of sight. When it was quite gone the warden picked his gun up and holstered it, dragged the doe behind some bushes, and started to walk back along the highway towards the crest of the grade.

## 6

The girl at the desk in the Kenworthy said: "This man called you three times, Lieutenant, but he wouldn't give a number. A lady called twice. Wouldn't leave name or number."

Delaguerra took three slips of paper from her, read the name "Joey Chill" on them and the various times. He picked up a couple of letters, touched his cap to the desk girl and got into the automatic elevator. He got off at four, walked down a narrow, quiet corridor, unlocked a door. Without switching on any lights he went across to a big french window, opened it wide, stood there looking at the thick dark sky, the flash of neon lights, the stabbing beams of headlamps on Ortega Boulevard, two blocks over.

He lit a cigarette and smoked half of it without moving. His face in the dark was very long, very troubled. Finally he left the window and went into a small bedroom, switched on a table lamp and undressed to the skin. He got under the shower, toweled himself, put on clean linen and went into the kitchenette to mix a drink. He sipped that and smoked another cigarette while he finished dressing. The telephone in the living room rang as he was strapping on his holster.

It was Belle Marr. Her voice was blurred and throaty, as if she had been crying for hours.

"I'm so glad to get you, Sam. I—I didn't mean the way I talked. I was shocked and confused, absolutely wild inside. You knew that, didn't you, Sam?"

"Sure, kid," Delaguerra said. "Think nothing of it. Anyway you were right. I just got back from Puma Lake and I think I was just sent up there to get rid of me."

"You're all I have now, Sam. You won't let them hurt you, will you?"

"Who?"

"You know. I'm no fool, Sam. I know this was all a plot, a vile political plot to get rid of him."

Delaguerra held the phone very tight. His mouth felt stiff and hard. For a moment he couldn't speak. Then he said: "It might be just what it looks like, Belle. A quarrel over those pictures. After all Donny had a right to tell a guy like that to get off the ticket. That wasn't blackmail . . . And he had a gun in his hand, you know."

"Come out and see me when you can, Sam." Her voice lingered with a spent emotion, a note of wistfulness.

He drummed on the desk, hesitated again, said: "Sure . . . When was anybody at Puma Lake last, at the cabin?"

"I don't know. I haven't been there in a year. He went . . . alone. Perhaps he met people there. I don't know."

He said something vaguely, after a moment said goodbye and hung up. He stared at the wall over the writing desk. There was a fresh light in his eyes, a hard glint. His whole face was tight, not doubtful any more.

He went back to the bedroom for his coat and straw hat. On the way out he picked up the three telephone slips with the name "Joey Chill" on them, tore them into small pieces and burned the pieces in an ash tray.

# 7

Pete Marcus, the big, sandy-haired dick, sat sidewise at a small littered desk in a bare office in which there were two such desks, faced to opposite walls. The other desk was neat and tidy, had a green blotter with an onyx pen set, a small brass calendar and an abalone shell for an ash tray.

A round straw cushion that looked something like a target was propped on end in a straight chair by the window. Pete Marcus had a handful of bank pens in his left hand and he was flipping them at the cushion, like a Mexican knife thrower. He was doing it absently, without much skill.

The door opened and Delaguerra came in. He shut the door and leaned against it, looking woodenly at Marcus. The sandy-haired man creaked his chair around and tilted it back against the desk, scratched his chin with a broad thumbnail.

"Hi, Spanish. Nice trip? The Chief's yappin' for you."

Delaguerra grunted, stuck a cigarette between his smooth brown lips.

"Were you in Marr's office when those photos were found, Pete?"

"Yeah, but I didn't find them. The Commish did. Why?"

"Did you see him find them?"

Marcus stared a moment, then said quietly, guardedly: "He found them all right, Sam. He didn't plant them—if that's what you mean."

Delaguerra nodded, shrugged. "Anything on the slugs?"

"Yeah. Not thirty-twos—twenty-fives. A damn vest-pocket rod. Copper-nickel slugs. An automatic, though, and we didn't find any shells."

"Imlay remembered those," Delaguerra said evenly, "but he left without the photos he killed for."

Marcus lowered his feet to the floor and leaned forward, looking up past his tawny eyebrows.

"That could be. They give him a motive, but with the gun in Marr's hand they kind of knock a premeditation angle."

"Good headwork, Pete." Delaguerra walked over to the small window, stood looking out of it. After a moment Marcus said dully: "You don't see me doin' any work, do you, Spanish?"

Delaguerra turned slowly, went over and stood close to Marcus, looking down at him.

"Don't be sore, kid. You're my partner, and I'm tagged as Marr's line into Headquarters. You're getting some of that. You're sitting still and I was hiked up to Puma Lake for no good reason except to have a deer carcass planted in the back of my car and have a game warden nick me with it."

Marcus stood up very slowly, knotting his fists at his sides. His heavy gray eyes opened very wide. His big nose was white at the nostrils.

"Nobody here'd go *that* far, Sam."

Delaguerra shook his head. "I don't think so either. But they could take a hint to send me up there. And somebody outside the department could do the rest."

Pete Marcus sat down again. He picked up one of the pointed bank pens and flipped it viciously at the round straw cushion. The point stuck, quivered, broke, and the pen rattled to the floor.

"Listen," he said thickly, not looking up, "this is a job to me. That's all it is. A living. I don't have any ideals about this police work like you have. Say the word and I'll heave the goddamn badge in the old boy's puss."

Delaguerra bent down, punched him in the ribs. "Skip it, copper. I've got ideas. Go on home and get drunk."

He opened the door and went out quickly, walked along a marble-faced corridor to a place where it widened into an alcove with three doors. The middle one said: CHIEF OF DETECTIVES. ENTER. Delaguerra went into a small reception room with a plain railing across it. A police stenographer behind the railing looked up, then jerked his head at an inner door. Delaguerra opened a gate in the railing and knocked at the inner door, then went in.

Two men were in the big office. Chief of Detectives Tod McKim sat behind a heavy desk, looked at Delaguerra hard-eyed as he came in. He was a big, loose man who had gone saggy. He had a long, petulantly melancholy face. One of his eyes was not quite straight in his head.

The man who sat in a round-backed chair at the end of the desk was dandyishly dressed, wore spats. A pearl-gray hat and gray gloves and an ebony cane lay beside him on another chair. He had a shock of soft white hair and a handsome dissipated face kept pink by constant massaging. He smiled at Delaguerra, looked vaguely amused and ironical, smoked a cigarette in a long amber holder.

Delaguerra sat down opposite McKim. Then he looked at the white-haired man briefly and said: "Good evening, Commissioner."

Commissioner Drew nodded offhandedly, didn't speak.

McKim leaned forward and clasped blunt, nail-chewed fingers on the shiny desk top. He said quietly: "Took your time reporting back. Find anything?"

Delaguerra stared at him, a level expressionless stare. "I wasn't meant to—except maybe a doe carcass in the back of my car."

Nothing changed in McKim's face. Not a muscle of it moved. Drew dragged a pink and polished fingernail across the front of his throat and made a tearing sound with his tongue and teeth.

"That's no crack to be makin' at your boss, lad."

Delaguerra kept on looking at McKim, waited. McKim spoke slowly, sadly: "You've got a good record, Delaguerra. Your grandfather was one of the best sheriffs this county ever had. You've blown a lot of dirt on it today. You're charged with violating game laws, interfering with a Toluca County officer in the performance of his duty, and resisting arrest. Got anything to say to all that?"

Delaguerra said tonelessly: "Is there a tag out for me?"

McKim shook his head very slowly. "It's a department charge. There's no formal complaint. Lack of evidence, I guess." He smiled dryly, without humor.

Delaguerra said quietly: "In that case I guess you'll want my badge."

McKim nodded, silent. Drew said: "You're a little quick on the trigger. Just a shade fast on the snap-up."

Delaguerra took his badge out, rubbed it on his

sleeve, looked at it, pushed it across the smooth wood of the desk.

"Okey, Chief," he said very softly. "My blood is Spanish, pure Spanish. Not nigger-Mex and not Yaqui-Mex. My grandfather would have handled a situation like this with fewer words and more powder smoke, but that doesn't mean I think it's funny. I've been deliberately framed into this spot because I was a close friend of Donegan Marr once. You know and I know that never counted for anything on the job. The Commissioner and his political backers may not feel so sure."

Drew stood up suddenly. "By God, you'll not talk like that to me," he yelped.

Delaguerra smiled slowly. He said nothing, didn't look towards Drew at all. Drew sat down again, scowling, breathing hard.

After a moment McKim scooped the badge into the middle drawer of his desk and got to his feet.

"You're suspended for a board, Delaguerra. Keep in touch with me." He went out of the room quickly, by the inner door, without looking back.

Delaguerra pushed his chair back and straightened his hat on his head. Drew cleared his throat, assumed a conciliatory smile and said: "Maybe I was a little hasty myself. The Irish in me. Have no hard feelings. The lesson you're learning is something we've all had to learn. Might I give you a word of advice?"

Delaguerra stood up, smiled at him, a small dry smile that moved the corners of his mouth and left the rest of his face wooden.

"I know what it is, Commissioner. Lay off the Marr case."

Drew laughed, good-humored again. "Not exactly. There isn't any Marr case. Imlay has admitted the shooting through his attorney, claiming self-defense.

He's to surrender in the morning. No, my advice was something else. Go back to Toluca County and tell the warden you're sorry. I think that's all that's needed. You might try it and see."

Delaguerra moved quietly to the corridor and opened it. Then he looked back with a sudden flashing grin that showed all his white teeth.

"I know a crook when I see one, Commissioner. He's been paid for his trouble already."

He went out. Drew watched the door close shut with a faint whoosh, a dry click. His face was stiff with rage. His pink skin had turned a doughy gray. His hand shook furiously, holding the amber holder, and ash fell on the knee of his immaculate knife-edged trousers.

"By God," he said rigidly, in the silence, "you may be a damn-smooth Spaniard. You may be smooth as plate glass—but you're a hell of a lot easier to poke a hole through!"

He rose, awkward with anger, brushed the ashes from his trousers carefully and reached a hand out for hat and cane. The manicured fingers of the hand were trembling.

# 8

Newton Street, between Third and Fourth, was a block of cheap clothing stores, pawnshops, arcades of slot machines, mean hotels in front of which furtive-eyed men slid words delicately along their cigarettes, without moving their lips. Midway of the block a jutting wooden sign on a canopy said, STOLL'S BILLIARD PARLORS. Steps went down from the sidewalk edge. Delaguerra went down the steps.

It was almost dark in the front of the poolroom. The tables were sheeted, the cues racked in rigid lines. But there was light far at the back, hard white light against which clustered heads and shoulders were silhouetted. There was noise, wrangling, shouting of odds. Delaguerra went towards the light.

Suddenly, as if at a signal, the noise stopped and out of the silence came the sharp click of balls, the dull thud of cue ball against cushion after cushion, the final click of a three-bank carom. Then the noise flared up again.

Delaguerra stopped beside a sheeted table and got a ten-dollar bill from his wallet, got a small gummed label from a pocket in the wallet. He wrote on it: "Where is Joe?" pasted it to the bill, folded the bill in four. He went on to the fringe of the crowd and inched his way through until he was close to the table.

A tall, pale man with an impassive face and neatly parted brown hair was chalking a cue, studying the set-up on the table. He leaned over, bridged with strong white fingers. The betting ring noise dropped like a stone. The tall man made a smooth, effortless three-cushion shot.

A chubby-faced man on a high stool intoned: "Forty for Chill. Eight's the break."

The tall man chalked his cue again, looked around idly. His eyes passed over Delaguerra without sign. Delaguerra stepped closer to him, said: "Back yourself, Max? Five-spot against the next shot."

The tall man nodded. "Take it."

Delaguerra put the folded bill on the edge of the table. A youth in a striped shirt reached for it. Max Chill blocked him off without seeming to, tucked the bill in a pocket of his vest, said tonelessly: "Five bet," and bent to make another shot.

It was a clean crisscross at the top of the table, a hairline shot. There was a lot of applause. The tall man handed his cue to his helper in the striped shirt, said: "Time out. I got to go a place."

He went back through the shadows, through a door marked MEN. Delaguerra lit a cigarette, looked around at the usual Newton Street riffraff. Max Chill's opponent, another tall, pale, impassive man, stood beside the marker and talked to him without looking at him. Near them, alone and supercilious, a very good-looking Filipino in a smart tan suit was puffing at a chocolate-colored cigarette.

Max Chill came back to the table, reached for his cue, chalked it. He reached a hand into his vest, said lazily: "Owe you five, buddy," passed a folded bill to Delaguerra.

He made three caroms in a row, almost without stopping. The marker said: "Forty-four for Chill. Twelve's the break."

Two men detached themselves from the edge of the crowd, started towards the entrance. Delaguerra fell in behind them, followed them among the sheeted tables to the foot of the steps. He stopped there, unfolded the bill in his hand, read the address scribbled on the label under his question. He crumpled the bill in his hand, started it towards his pocket.

Something hard poked into his back. A twangy voice like a plucked banjo string said: "Help a guy out, huh?"

Delaguerra's nostrils quivered, got sharp. He looked up the steps at the legs of the two men ahead, at the reflected glare of street lights.

"Okey," the twangy voice said grimly.

Delaguerra dropped sidewise, twisting in the air. He shot a snakelike arm back. His hand grabbed an ankle as he fell. A swept gun missed his head, cracked the point of his shoulder and sent a dart of pain down his left arm. There was hard, hot breathing. Something without force slammed his straw hat. There was a thin tearing snarl close to him. He rolled, twisted the ankle, tucked a knee under him and lunged up. He was on his feet, catlike, lithe. He threw the ankle away from him, hard.

The Filipino in the tan suit hit the floor with his back. A gun wobbled up. Delaguerra kicked it out of a small brown hand and it skidded under a table. The Filipino lay still on his back, his head straining up, his snap-brim hat still glued to his oily hair.

At the back of the poolroom the three-cushion match went on peacefully. If anyone noticed the scuffling sound, at least no one moved to investigate. Delaguerra jerked a thonged blackjack from his hip pocket, bent over. The Filipino's tight brown face cringed.

"Got lots to learn. On the feet, baby."

Delaguerra's voice was chilled but casual. The dark man scrambled up, lifted his arms, then his left hand snaked for his right shoulder. The blackjack knocked it down, with a careless flip of Delaguerra's wrist. The brown man screamed thinly, like a hungry kitten.

Delaguerra shrugged. His mouth moved in a sardonic grin.

"Stick-up, huh? Okey, yellowpuss, some other time. I'm busy now. Dust!"

The Filipino slid back among the tables, crouched down. Delaguerra shifted the blackjack to his left hand, shot his right to a gun butt. He stood for a moment like that, watching the Filipino's eyes. Then he turned and went quickly up the steps, out of sight.

The brown man darted forward along the wall, crept under the table for his gun.

# 9

Joey Chill, who jerked the door open, held a short, worn gun without a foresight. He was a small man, hardbitten, with a tight, worried face. He needed a

shave and a clean shirt. A harsh animal smell came
out of the room behind him.

He lowered the gun, grinned sourly, stepped back
into the room.

"Okey, copper. Took your sweet time gettin' here."

Delaguerra went in and shut the door. He pushed
his straw hat far back on his wiry hair, and looked at
Joey Chill without any expression. He said: "Am I
supposed to remember the address of every punk in
town? I had to get it from Max."

The small man growled something and went and lay
down on the bed, shoved his gun under the pillow.
He clasped his hands behind his head and blinked at
the ceiling.

"Got a *C* note on you, copper?"

Delaguerra jerked a straight chair in front of the
bed and straddled it. He got his bulldog pipe out,
filled it slowly, looking with distaste at the shut window, the chipped enamel of the bed frame, the dirty,
tumbled bedclothes, the wash bowl in the corner with
two smeared towels hung over it, the bare dresser with
half a bottle of gin planked on top of the Gideon Bible.

"Holed up?" he inquired, without much interest.

"I'm hot, copper. I mean I'm hot. I got something
see. It's worth a *C* note."

Delaguerra put his pouch away slowly, indifferently,
held a lighted match to his pipe, puffed with exasperat-
ing leisure. The small man on the bed fidgeted, watching him with sidelong looks. Delaguerra said slowly:
"You're a good stoolie, Joey. I'll always say that for
you. But a hundred bucks is important money to a
copper."

"Worth it, guy. If you like the Marr killing well
enough to want to break it right."

Delaguerra's eyes got steady and very cold. His teeth

clamped on the pipe stem. He spoke very quietly, very grimly.

"I'll listen, Joey. I'll pay if it's worth it. It better be right, though."

The small man rolled over on his elbow. "Know who the girl was with Imlay in thos pajama-pajama snaps?"

"Know her name," Delaguerra said evenly. "I haven't seen the pictures."

"Stella La Motte's a hoofer name. Real name Stella Chill. My kid sister."

Delaguerra folded his arms on the back of the chair. "That's nice," he said. "Go on."

"She framed him, copper. Framed him for a few bindles of heroin from a slant-eyed Flip."

"Flip?" Delaguerra spoke the word swiftly, harshly. His face was tense now.

"Yeah, a little brown brother. A looker, a neat dresser, a snow peddler. A goddamn dodo. Name, Toribo. They call him the Caliente Kid. He had a place across the hall from Stella. He got to feedin' her the stuff. Then he works her into the frame. She puts heavy drops in Imlay's liquor and he passes out. She lets the Flip in to shoot pictures with a Minny camera. Cute, huh? . . . And then, just like a broad, she gets sorry and spills the whole thing to Max and me."

Delaguerra nodded, silent, almost rigid.

The little man grinned sharply, showed his small teeth. "What do I do? I take a plant on the Flip. I live in his shadow, copper. And after a while I tail him bang into Dave Aage's skyline apartment in the Vendome . . . I guess that rates a yard."

Delaguerra nodded slowly, shook a little ash into the palm of his hand and blew it off. "Who else knows this?"

"Max. He'll back me up, if you handle him right. Only he don't want any part of it. He don't play those games. He gave Stella dough to leave town and signed off. Because those boys are tough."

"Max couldn't know where you followed the Filipino to, Joey."

The small man sat up sharply, swung his feet to the floor. His face got sullen.

"I'm not kidding you, copper. I never have."

Delaguerra said quietly, "I believe you, Joey. I'd like more proof, though. What do you make of it?"

The little man snorted. "Hell, it sticks up so hard it hurts. Either the Flip's working for Masters and Aage before or he makes a deal with them after he gets the snaps. Then Marr gets the pictures and it's a cinch he don't get them unless they say so and he don't know they had them. Imlay was running for judge, on their ticket. Okey, he's their punk, but he's still a punk. It happens he's a guy who drinks and has a nasty temper. That's known."

Delaguerra's eyes glistened a little. The rest of his face was like carved wood. The pipe in his mouth was as motionless as though set in cement.

Joey Chill went on, with his sharp little grin: "So they deal the big one. They get the pictures to Marr without Marr's knowing where they came from. Then Imlay gets tipped off who has them, what they are, that Marr is set to put the squeeze on him. What would a guy like Imlay do? He'd go hunting, copper—and Big John Masters and his sidekick would eat the ducks."

"Or the venison," Delaguerra said absently.

"Huh? Well, does it rate?"

Delaguerra reached for his wallet, shook the money out of it, counted some bills on his knee. He rolled them into a tight wad and flipped them on to the bed.

"I'd like a line to Stella pretty well, Joey. How about it?"

The small man stuffed the money in his shirt pocket, shook his head. "No can do. You might try Max again. I think she's left town, and me, I'm doin' that too, now I've got the scratch. Because those boys are tough like I said—and maybe I didn't tail so good . . . Because some mugg's been tailin' me." He stood up, yawned, added: "Snort of gin?"

Delaguerra shook his head, watched the little man go over to the dresser and lift the gin bottle, pour a big dose into a thick glass. He drained the glass, started to put it down.

Glass tinkled at the window. There was a sound like the loose slap of a glove. A small piece of the window glass dropped to the bare stained wood beyond the carpet, almost at Joey Chill's feet.

The little man stood quite motionless for two or three seconds. Then the glass fell from his hand, bounced and rolled against the wall. Then his legs gave. He went down on his side, slowly, rolled slowly over on his back.

Blood began to move sluggishly down his cheek from a hole over his left eye. It moved faster. The hole got large and red. Joey Chill's eyes looked blankly at the ceiling, as if those things no longer concerned him at all.

Delaguerra slipped quietly down out of the chair to his hands and knees. He crawled along the side of the bed, over to the wall by the window, reached out from there and groped inside Joey Chill's shirt. He held fingers against his heart for a little while, took them away, shook his head. He squatted down low, took his hat off, and pushed his head up very carefully until he could see over a lower corner of the window.

He looked at the high blank wall of a storage warehouse, across an alley. There were scattered windows in it, high up, none of them lighted. Delaguerra pulled his head down again, said quietly, under his breath: "Silenced rifle, maybe. And very sweet shooting."

His hand went forward again, diffidently, took the little roll of bills from Joey Chill's shirt. He went back along the wall to the door, still crouched, reached up and got the key from the door, opened it, straightened and stepped through quickly, locked the door from the outside.

He went along a dirty corridor and down four flights of steps to a narrow lobby. The lobby was empty. There was a desk and a bell on it, no one behind it. Delaguerra stood behind the plate-glass street door and looked across the street at a frame rooming house where a couple of old men rocked on the porch, smoking. They looked very peaceful. He watched them for a couple of minutes.

He went out, searched both sides of the block quickly with sharp glances, walked along beside parked cars to the next corner. Two blocks over he picked up a cab and rode back to Stoll's Billiard Parlors on Newton Street.

Lights were lit all over the poolroom now. Balls clicked and spun, players weaved in and out of a thick haze of cigarette smoke. Delaguerra looked around, then went to where a chubby-faced man sat on a high stool beside a cash register.

"You Stoll?"

The chubby-faced man nodded.

"Where did Max Chill get to?"

"Long gone, brother. They only played a hundred up. Home, I guess."

"Where's home?"

The chubby-faced man gave him a swift, flickering glance that passed like a finger of light.

"I wouldn't know."

Delaguerra lifted a hand to the pocket where he

carried his badge. He dropped it again—tried not to drop it too quickly. The chubby-faced man grinned.

"Flattie, eh? Okey, he lives at the Mansfield, three blocks west on Grand."

# 10

Cefarino Toribo, the good-looking Filipino in the well-cut tan suit, gathered two dimes and three pennies off the counter in the telegraph office, smiled at the bored blonde who was waiting on him.

"That goes out right away, Sugar?"

She glanced at the message icily. "Hotel Mansfield? Be there in twenty minutes—and save the sugar."

"Okey, Sugar."

Toribo dawdled elegantly out of the office. The blonde spiked the message with a jab, said over her shoulder: "Guy must be nuts. Sending a wire to a hotel three blocks away."

Ceferino Toribo strolled along Spring Street, trailing smoke over his neat shoulder from a chocolate-colored cigarette. At Fourth he turned west, went three blocks more, turned into the side entrance of the Mansfield, by the barbershop. He went up some marble steps to a mezzanine, along the back of a writing room and up carpeted steps to the third floor. He passed the elevators and swaggered down a long corridor to the end, looking at the numbers on doors.

He came back halfway to the elevators, sat down in an open space where there was a pair of windows on the court, a glass-topped table and chairs. He lit a fresh cigarette from his stub, leaned back and listened to the elevators.

He leaned forward sharply whenever one stopped at that floor, listening for steps. The steps came in something over ten minutes. He stood up and went to the corner of the wall where the widened-out space began. He took a long thin gun out from under his right arm, transferred it to his right hand, held it down against the wall beside his leg.

A squat, pockmarked Filipino in bellhop's uniform came along the corridor, carrying a small tray. Toribo made a hissing noise, lifted the gun. The squat Filipino whirled. His mouth opened and his eyes bulged at the gun.

Toribo said, "What room, punk?"

The squat Filipino smiled very nervously, placatingly. He came close, showed Toribo a yellow envelope on his tray. The figures 338 were penciled on the window of the envelope.

"Put it down," Toribo said calmly.

The squat Filipino put the telegram on the table. He kept his eyes on the gun.

"Beat it," Toribo said. "You put it under the door, see?"

The squat Filipino ducked his round black head, smiled nervously again, and went away very quicky towards the elevators.

Toribo put the gun in his jacket pocket, took out a folded white paper. He opened it very carefully, shook glistening white powder from it on to the hollow place formed between his left thumb and forefinger when he spread his hand. He sniffed the powder sharply up his nose, took out a flame-colored silk handkerchief and wiped his nose.

He stood still for a little while. His eyes got the dullness of slate and the skin on his brown face seemed to tighten over his high cheekbones. He breathed audibly between his teeth.

He picked the yellow envelope up and went along the corridor to the end, stopped in front of the last door, knocked.

A voice called out. He put his lips close to the door, spoke in a high-pitched, very deferential voice.

"Mail for you, sar."

Bedsprings creaked. Steps came across the floor inside. A key turned and the door opened. Toribo had his thin gun out again by this time. As the door opened he stepped swiftly into the opening, sidewise, with a graceful sway of his hips. He put the muzzle of the thin gun against Max Chill's abdomen.

"Back up!" he snarled, and his voice now had the metallic twang of a plucked banjo string.

Max Chill backed away from the gun. He backed across the room to the bed, sat down on the bed when his legs struck the side of it. Springs creaked and a newspaper rustled. Max Chill's pale face under the neatly parted brown hair had no expression at all.

Toribo shut the door softly, snapped the lock. When the door latch snapped, Max Chill's face suddenly became a sick face. His lips began to shake, kept on shaking.

Toribo said mockingly, in his twangy voice: "You talk to the cops, huh? *Adios.*"

The thin gun jumped in his hand, kept on jumping. A little pale smoke lisped from the muzzle. The noise the gun made was no louder than a hammer striking a nail or knuckles rapping sharply on wood. It made that noise seven times.

Max Chill lay down on the bed very slowly. His feet stayed on the floor. His eyes went blank, and his lips parted and a pinkish froth seethed on them. Blood showed in several places on the front of his loose shirt. He lay quite still on his back and looked at the ceiling with his feet touching the floor and the pink froth bubbling on his blue lips.

Toribo moved the gun to his left hand and put it away under his arm. He sidled over to the bed and stood beside it, looking down at Max Chill. After a while the pink froth stopped bubbling and Max Chill's face became the quiet, empty face of a dead man.

Toribo went back to the door, opened it, started to back out, his eyes still on the bed. There was a stir of movement behind him.

He started to whirl, snatching a hand up. Something looped at his head. The floor tilted queerly before his eyes, rushed up at his face. He didn't know when it struck his face.

Delaguerra kicked the Filipino's legs into the room, out of the way of the door. He shut the door, locked it, walked stiffly over to the bed, swinging a thonged sap at his side. He stood beside the bed for quite a long time. At last he said under his breath: "They clean up. Yeah—they clean up."

He went back to the Filipino, rolled him over and went through his pockets. There was a well-lined wallet without any identification, a gold lighter set with garnets, a gold cigarette case, keys, a gold pencil and knife, the flame-colored handkerchief, loose money, two guns and spare clips for them, and five bindles of heroin powder in the ticket pocket of the tan jacket.

He left it thrown around on the floor, stood up. The Filipino breathed heavily, with his eyes shut, a muscle twitching in one cheek. Delaguerra took a coil of thin wire out of his pocket and wired the brown man's wrists behind him. He dragged him over to the bed, sat him up against the leg, looped a strand of the wire around his neck and around the bed post. He tied the flame-colored handkerchief to the looped wire.

He went into the bathroom and got a glass of water and threw it into the Filipino's face as hard as he could throw it.

Toribo jerked, gagged sharply as the wire caught his

neck. His eyes jumped open. He opened his mouth to yell.

Delaguerra jerked the wire taut against the brown throat. The yell was cut off as though by a switch. There was a strained anguished gurgle. Toribo's mouth drooled.

Delaguerra let the wire go slack again and put his head down close to the Filipino's head. He spoke to him gently, with a dry, very deadly gentleness.

"You want to talk to me, spig. Maybe not right away, maybe not even soon. But after a while you want to talk to me."

The Filipino's eyes rolled yellowly. He spat. Then his lips came together, tight.

Delaguerra smiled a faint, grim smile. "Tough boy," he said softly. He jerked the handkerchief back, held it tight and hard, biting into the brown throat above the adam's apple.

The Filipino's legs began to jump on the floor. His body moved in sudden lunges. The brown of his face became a thick congested purple. His eyes bulged, shot with blood,

Delaguerra let the wire go loose again.

The Filipino gasped air into his lungs. His head sagged, then jerked back against the bedpost. He shook with a chill.

"Sí . . . I talk," he breathed.

## 11

When the bell rang Ironhead Toomey very carefully put a black ten down on a red jack. Then he licked his lips and put all the cards down and looked around towards the front door of the bungalow, through the dining-room arch. He stood up slowly, a big brute of a man with loose gray hair and a big nose.

In the living room beyond the arch a thin blonde girl was lying on a davenport, reading a magazine under a lamp with a torn red shade. She was pretty, but too pale, and her thin, high-arched eyebrows gave her face a startled look. She put the magazine down and swung her feet to the floor and looked at Ironhead Toomey with sharp, sudden fear in her eyes.

Toomey jerked his thumb silently. The girl stood up and went very quickly through the arch and through a swing door into the kitchen. She shut the swing door slowly, so that it made no noise.

The bell rang again, longer. Toomey shoved his white-socked feet into carpet slippers, hung a pair of glasses on his big nose, took a revolver off a chair beside him. He picked a crumpled newspaper off the floor and arranged it loosely in front of the gun, which he held in his left hand. He strolled unhurriedly to the front door.

He was yawning as he opened it, peering with sleepy eyes through the glasses at the tall man who stood on the porch.

"Okey," he said wearily. "Talk it up."

Delaguerra said: "I'm a police officer. I want to see Stella La Motte."

Ironhead Toomey put an arm like a Yule log across the door frame and leaned solidly against it. His expression remained bored.

"Wrong dump, copper. No broads here."

Delaguerra said: "I'll come in and look."

Toomey said cheerfully: "You will—like hell."

Delaguerra jerked a gun out of his pocket very smoothly and swiftly, smashed it at Toomey's left wrist. The newspaper and the big revolver fell down on the floor of the porch. Toomey's face got a less bored expression.

"Old gag," Delaguerra snapped. "Let's go in."

Toomey shook his left wrist, took his other arm off the door frame and swung hard at Delaguerra's jaw. Delaguerra moved his head about four inches. He frowned, made a disapproving noise with his tongue and lips.

Toomey dived at him. Delaguerra sidestepped and chopped the gun at a big gray head. Toomey landed on his stomach, half in the house and half out on the porch. He grunted, planted his hands firmly and started to get up again, as if nothing had hit him.

Delaguerra kicked Toomey's gun out of the way. A swing door inside the house made a light sound. Toomey was up on one knee and one hand as Delaguerra looked towards the noise. He took a swing at Delaguerra's stomach, hit him. Delaguerra grunted and hit Toomey on the head again, hard. Toomey shook his head, growled: "Sappin' me is a waste of time, bo."

He dived sidewise, got hold of Delaguerra's leg, jerked the leg off the floor. Delaguerra sat down on the boards of the porch, jammed in the doorway. His head hit the side of the doorway, dazed him.

The thin blonde rushed through the arch with a small automatic in her hand. She pointed it at Delaguerra, said furiously: "Reach, damn you!"

Delaguerra shook his head, started to say something, then caught his breath as Toomey twisted his foot. Toomey set his teeth hard and twisted the foot as if he was all alone in the world with it and it was his foot and he could do what he liked with it.

Delaguerra's head jerked back again and his face got white. His mouth twisted into a harsh grimace of pain. He heaved up, grabbed Toomey's hair with is left hand, dragged the big head up and over until his chin came up, straining. Delaguerra smashed the barrel of his Colt on the skin.

Toomey became limp, an inert mass, fell across his

legs and pinned him to the floor. Delaguerra couldn't move. He was propped on the floor on his right hand, trying to keep from being pushed flat by Toomey's weight. He couldn't get his right hand with the gun in it off the floor. The blonde was closer to him now, wild-eyed, white-faced with rage.

Delaguerra said in a spent voice. "Don't be a fool, Stella. Joey——"

The blonde's face was unnatural. Her eyes were unnatural, with small pupils, a queer flat glitter in them.

"Cops!" she almost screamed. "Cops! God, how I hate cops!"

The gun in her hand crashed. The echoes of it filled the room, went out of the open front door, died against the highboard fence across the street.

A sharp blow like the blow of a club hit the left side of Delaguerra's head. Pain filled his head. Light flared—blinding white light that filled the world. Then it was dark. He fell soundlessly, into bottomless darkness.

# 12

Light came back as a red fog in front of his eyes. Hard, bitter pain racked the side of his head, his whole face, ground in his teeth. His tongue was hot and thick when he tried to move it. He tried to move his hands. They were far away from him, not his hands at all.

Then he opened his eyes and the red fog went away and he was looking at a face. It was a big face, very close to him, a huge face. It was fat and had sleek blue jowls and there was a cigar with a bright band in a grinning, thick-lipped mouth. The face chuckled. Delaguerra closed his eyes again and the pain washed over him, submerged him. He passed out.

Seconds, or years, passed. He was looking at the face again. He heard a thick voice.

"Well, he's with us again. A pretty tough lad at that."

The face came closer, the end of the cigar glowed cherry-red. Then he was coughing rackingly, gagging on smoke. The side of his head seemed to burst open. He felt fresh blood slide down his cheekbone, tickling the skin, then slide over stiff dried blood that had already caked on his face.

"That fixes him up swell," the thick voice said.

Another voice with a touch of brogue to it said something gentle and obscene. The big face whirled towards the sound, snarling.

Delaguerra came wide awake then. He saw the room clearly, saw the four people in it. The big face was the face of Big John Masters.

The thin blonde girl was hunched on one end of the davenport, staring at the floor with a doped expression, her arms stiff at her sides, her hands out of sight in the cushions.

Dave Aage had his long lank body propped against a wall beside a curtained window. His wedge-shaped face looked bored. Commissioner Drew was on the other end of the davenport, under the frayed lamp. The light made silver in his hair. His blue eyes were very bright, very intent.

There was a shiny gun in Big John Masters' hand. Delaguerra blinked at it, started to get up. A hard hand jerked at his chest, jarred him back. A wave of nausea went over him. The thick voice said harshly: "Hold it, pussyfoot. You've had your fun. This is our party."

Delaguerra licked his lips, said: "Give me a drink of water."

Dave Aage stood away from the wall and went through the dining-room arch. He came back with a glass, held it to Delaguerra's mouth. Delaguerra drank.

Masters said: "We like your guts, copper. But you don't use them right. It seems you're a guy that can't take a hint. That's too bad. That makes you through. Get me?"

The blonde turned her head and looked at Delaguerra with heavy eyes, looked away again. Aage went back to his wall. Drew began to stroke the side of his face with quick nervous fingers, as if Delaguerra's bloody head made his own face hurt. Delaguerra said slowly: "Killing me will just hang you a little higher, Masters. A sucker on the big time is still a sucker. You've had two men killed already for no reason at all. You don't even know what you're trying to cover."

The big man swore harshly, jerked the shiny gun up, then lowered it slowly, with a heavy leer. Aage said indolently: "Take it easy, John. Let him speak his piece."

Delaguerra said in the same slow, careless voice: "The lady over there is the sister of the two men you've had killed. She told them her story, about framing Imlay, who got the pictures, how they got to Donegan Marr. Your little Filipino hood has done some singing. I get the general idea all right. You couldn't be sure Imlay would kill Marr. Maybe Marr would get Imlay. It would work out all right either way. Only, if Imlay did kill Marr, the case had to be broken fast. That's where you slipped. You started to cover up before you really knew what happened."

Masters said harshly: "Crummy, copper, crummy. You're wasting my time."

The blonde turned her head towards Delaguerra, towards Masters' back. There was hard green hate in her eyes now. Delaguerra shrugged very slightly, went on: "It was routine stuff for you to put killers on the Chill brothers. It was routine stuff to get me off the investigation, get me framed, and suspended because you figured I was on Marr's payroll. But it wasn't routine when you couldn't find Imlay—and that crowded you."

Masters' hard black eyes got wide and empty. His thick neck swelled. Aage came away from the wall a few feet and stood rigidly. After a moment Masters snapped his teeth, spoke very quietly: "That's a honey, copper. Tell us about that one."

Delaguerra touched his smeared face with the tips of two fingers, looked at the fingers. His eyes were depthless, ancient.

"Imlay is dead, Masters. He was dead before Marr was killed."

The room was very still. Nobody moved in it. The four people Delaguerra looked at were frozen with shock. After a long time Masters drew in a harsh breath and blew it out and almost whispered: "Tell it, copper. Tell it fast, or by God I'll——"

Delaguerra's voice cut in on him coldly, without any emotion at all: "Imlay went to see Marr all right. Why wouldn't he? He didn't know he was double-crossed. Only he went to see him last night, not today. He rode up to the cabin at Puma Lake with him, to talk things over in a friendly way. That was the gag, anyhow. Then, up there, they had their fight and Imlay got killed, got dumped off the end of the porch, got his head smashed open on some rocks. He's dead as last Christmas, in the woodshed of Marr's cabin . . . Okey, Marr hid him and came back to town. Then today he got a phone call, mentioning the name Imlay, making a date for twelve-fifteen. What would Marr do? Stall, of course, send his office girl off to lunch, put a gun where he could reach it in a hurry. He was all set for trouble then. Only the visitor fooled him and he didn't use the gun."

Masters said gruffly: "Hell, man, you're just cracking wise. You couldn't know all those things."

He looked back at Drew. Drew was gray-faced, taut. Aage came a little farther away from the wall and stood close to Drew. The blonde girl didn't move a muscle.

Delaguerra said wearily: "Sure, I'm guessing, but I'm guessing to fit the facts. It had to be like that. Marr was no slouch with a gun and he was on edge, all set. Why didn't he get a shot in? Because it was a woman that called on him."

He lifted an arm, pointed at the blonde. "There's your killer. She loved Imlay even though she framed him. She's a junkie and junkies are like that. She got sad and sorry and she went after Marr herself. Ask her!"

The blonde stood up in a smooth lunge. Her right hand jerked up from the cushions with a small automatic in it, the one she had shot Delaguerra with. Her green eyes were pale and empty and staring. Masters whirled around, flailed at her arm with the shiny revolver.

She shot him twice, point-blank, without a flicker of hesitation. Blood spurted from the side of his thick neck, down the front of his coat. He staggered, dropped the shiny revolver, almost at Delaguerra's feet. He fell outwards towards the wall behind Delaguerra's chair, one arm groping out for the wall. His hand hit the wall and trailed down it as he fell. He crashed heavily, didn't move again.

Delaguerra had the shiny revolver almost in his hand.

Drew was on his feet yelling. The girl turned slowly towards Aage, seemed to ignore Delaguerra. Aage jerked a Luger from under his arm and knocked Drew out of the way with his arm. The small automatic and the Luger roared at the same time. The small gun missed. The girl was flung down on the davenport, her left hand clutching at her breast. She rolled her eyes, tried to lift the gun again. Then she fell sidewise on the cushions and her left hand went lax, dropped away from her breast. The front of her dress was a sudden welter of blood. Her eyes opened and shut, opened and stayed open.

Aage swung the Luger towards Delaguerra. His eyebrows were twisted up into a sharp grin of intense strain. His smoothly combed, sand-colored hair flowed down his bony scalp as tightly as though it were painted on it.

Delaguerra shot him four times, so rapidly that the explosions were like the rattle of a machine gun.

In the instant of time before he fell Aage's face became the thin, empty face of an old man, his eyes the vacant eyes of an idiot. Then his long body jack-knifed to the floor, the Luger still in his hand. One leg doubled under him as if there was no bone in it.

Powder smell was sharp in the air. The air was stunned by the sound of guns. Delaguerra got to his feet slowly, motioned to Drew with the shiny revolver.

"Your party, Commissioner. Is this anything like what you wanted?"

Drew nodded slowly, white-faced, quivering. He swallowed, moved slowly across the floor, past Aage's sprawled body. He looked down at the girl on the davenport, shook his head. He went over to Masters, went down on one knee, touched him. He stood up again.

"All dead, I think," he muttered.

Delaguerra said: "That's swell. What happened to the big boy? The bruiser?"

"They sent him away. I—I don't think they meant to kill you, Delaguerra."

Delaguerra nodded a little. His face began to soften, the rigid lines began to go out of it. The side that was

not a bloodstained mask began to look human again.
He sopped at his face with a handkerchief. It came
away bright red with blood. He threw it away and
lightly fingered his matted hair into place. Some of it
was caught in the dried blood.

"The hell they didn't," he said.

The house was very still. There was no noise outside. Drew listened, sniffed, went to the front door and
looked out. The street outside was dark, silent. He
came back close to Delaguerra. Very slowly a smile
worked itself on to his face.

"It's a hell of a note," he said, "when a commissioner
of police has to be his own undercover man—and a
square cop had to be framed off the force to help
him."

Delaguerra looked at him without expression. "You
want to play it that way?"

Drew spoke calmly now. The pink was back in his
face. "For the good of the department, man, and the
city—and ourselves, it's the only way to play it."

Delaguerra looked him straight in the eyes.

"I like it that way too," he said in a dead voice.
"If it gets played—*exactly* that way."

# 13

Marcus braked the car to a stop and grinned admiringly at the big tree-shaded house.

"Pretty nice," he said. "I could go for a long rest
there myself."

Delaguerra got out of the car slowly, as if he was
stiff and very tired. He was hatless, carried his straw
under his arm. Part of the left side of his head was
shaved and the shaved part covered by a thick pad of
gauze and tape, over the stitches. A wick of wiry

black hair stuck up over one edge of the bandage, with a ludicrous effect.

He said: "Yeah—but I'm not staying here, sap. Wait for me."

He went along the path of stones that wound through the grass. Trees speared long shadows across the lawn, through the morning sunlight. The house was very still, with drawn blinds, a dark wreath on the brass knocker. Delaguerra didn't go up to the door. He turned off along another path under the windows and went along the side of the house past the gladioli beds.

There were more trees at the back, more lawn, more flowers, more sun and shadow. There was a pond with water lilies in it and a big stone bullfrog. Beyond was a half-circle of lawn chairs around an iron table with a tile top. In one of the chairs Belle Marr sat.

She wore a black-and-white dress, loose and casual, and there was a wide-brimmed garden hat on her chestnut hair. She sat very still, looking into the distance across the lawn. Her face was white. The make-up glared on it.

She turned her head slowly, smiled a dull smile, motioned to a chair beside her. Delaguerra didn't sit down. He took his straw from under his arm, snapped a finger at the brim, said: "The case is closed. There'll be inquests, investigations, threats, a lot of people shouting their mouths off to horn in on the publicity, that sort of thing. The papers will play it big for a while. But underneath, on the record, it's closed. You can begin to try to forget it."

The girl looked at him suddenly, widened her vivid blue eyes, looked away again, over the grass.

"Is your head very bad, Sam?" she asked softly.

Delaguerra said: "No. It's fine . . . What I mean is the La Motte girl shot Masters—and she shot Donny. Aage shot her. I shot Aage. All dead, ring around the rosy. Just how Imlay got killed we'll not know ever, I guess. I can't see that it matters now."

Without looking up at him Belle Marr said quietly: "But how did you know it was Imlay up at the cabin? The paper said—" She broke off, shuddered suddenly.

He stared woodenly at the hat he was holding. "I didn't. I thought a woman shot Donny. It looked like a good hunch that was Imlay up at the lake. It fitted his description."

"How did you know it was a woman . . . that killed Donny?" Her voice had a lingering, half-whispered stillness.

"I just knew."

He walked away a few steps, stood looking at the trees. He turned slowly, came back, stood beside her chair again. His face was very weary.

"We had great times together—the three of us. You and Donny and I. Life seems to do nasty things to people. It's all gone now—all the good part."

Her voice was still a whisper saying: "Maybe not all gone, Sam. We must see a lot of each other, from now on."

A vague smile moved the corners of his lips, went away again. "It's my first frame-up," he said quietly. "I hope it will be my last."

Belle Marr's head jerked a little. Her hands took hold of the arms of the chair, looked white against the varnished wood. Her whole body seemed to get rigid.

After a moment Delaguerra reached in his pocket and something gold glittered in his hand. He looked down at it dully.

"Got the badge back," he said. "It's not quite as clean as it was. Clean as most, I suppose. I'll try to keep it that way." He put it back in his pocket.

Very slowly the girl stood up in front of him. She

lifted her chin, stared at him with a long level stare.
Her face was a mask of white plaster behind the rouge.

She said: "My God, Sam—I begin to understand."

Delaguerra didn't look at her face. He looked past
her shoulder at some vague spot in the distance. He
spoke vaguely, distantly.

"Sure . . . I thought it was a woman because it was
a small gun such as a woman would use. But not only
on that account. After I went up to the cabin I knew
Donny was primed for trouble and it wouldn't be
that easy for a man to get the drop on him. But it was
a perfect set-up for Imlay to have done it. Masters and
Aage assumed he'd done it and had a lawyer phone in
admitting he did it and promising to surrender him in
the morning. So it was natural for anyone who didn't
know Imlay was dead to fall in line. Besides, no cop
would expect a woman to pick up her shells.

"After I got Joey Chill's story I thought it might be
the La Motte girl. But I didn't think so when I said it
in front of her. That was dirty. It got her killed, in a
way. Though I wouldn't give much for her chances
anyway, with that bunch."

Belle Marr was still staring at him. The breeze blew
a wisp of her hair and that was the only thing about her
that moved.

He brought his eyes back from the distance, looked
at her gravely for a brief moment, looked away again.
He took a small bunch of keys out of his pocket, tossed
them down on the table.

"Three things were tough to figure until I got completely wise. The writing on the pad, the gun in
Donny's hand, the missing shells. Then I tumbled to
it. He didn't die right away. He had guts and he used
them to the last flicker—to protect somebody. The writing on the pad was a bit shaky. He wrote it after-
wards, when he was alone, dying. He had been think-

ing of Imlay and writing the name helped mess the trail. Then he got the gun out of his desk to die with it in his hand. That left the shells. I got that too, after a while.

"The shots were fired close, across the desk, and there were books on one end of the desk. The shells fell there, stayed on the desk where he could get them. He couldn't have got them off the floor. There's a key to the office on your ring. I went there last night, late. I found the shells in a humidor with his cigars. Nobody looked for them there. You only find what you expect to find, after all."

He stopped talking and rubbed the side of his face. After a moment he added: "Donny did the best he could—and then he died. It was a swell job—and I'm letting him get away with it."

Belle Marr opened her mouth slowly. A kind of babble came out of it first, then words, clear words.

"It wasn't just women, Sam. It was the kind of women he had." She shivered. "I'll go downtown now and give myself up."

Delaguerra said: "No. I told you I was letting him get away with it. Downtown they like it the way it is. It's swell politics. It gets the city out from under the Masters-Aage mob. It puts Drew on top for a little while, but he's too weak to last. So that doesn't matter . . . You're not going to do anything about any of it. You're going to do what Donny used his last strength to show he wanted. You're staying out. Goodbye."

He looked at her white shattered face once more, very quickly. Then he swung around, walked away over the lawn, past the pool with the lily pads and the stone bullfrog along the side of the house and out to the car.

Pete Marcus swung the door open. Delaguerra got in and sat down and put his head far back against the seat, slumped down in the car and closed his eyes. He said flatly: "Take it easy, Pete. My head hurts like hell."

Marcus started the car and turned into the street, drove slowly back along De Neve Lane towards town. The tree-shaded house disappeared behind them. The tall trees finally hid it.

When they were a long way from it Delaguerra opened his eyes again.

# I'LL BE WAITING

AT ONE O'CLOCK in the morning, Carl, the night porter, turned down the last of three table lamps in the main lobby of the Windermere Hotel. The blue carpet darkened a shade of two and the walls drew back into remoteness. The chairs filled with shadowy loungers. In the corners were memories like cobwebs.

Tony Reseck yawned. He put his head on one side and listened to the frail, twittery music from the radio room beyond a dim arch at the far side of the lobby. He frowned. That should be his radio room after one A.M. Nobody should be in it. That red-haired girl was spoiling his nights.

The frown passed and a miniature of a smile quirked at the corners of his lips. He sat relaxed, a short, pale, paunchy, middle-aged man with long, delicate fingers clasped on the elk's tooth on his watch chain; the long delicate fingers of a sleight-of-hand artist, fingers with shiny, molded nails and tapering first joints, fingers a little spatulate at the ends. Handsome fingers. Tony Reseck rubbed them gently together and there was peace in his quiet sea-gray eyes.

The frown came back on his face. The music annoyed him. He got up with a curious litheness, all in one piece, without moving his clasped hands from the watch chain. At one moment he was leaning back relaxed, and the next he was standing balanced on his feet, perfectly still, so that the movement of rising seemed to be a thing perfectly perceived, an error of vision. . . .

He walked with small, polished shoes delicately across the blue carpet and under the arch. The music was louder. It contained the hot, acid blare, the frenetic, jittering runs of a jam session. It was too loud. The red-haired girl sat there and stared silently at the fretted part of the big radio cabinet as though she could see the band with its fixed professional grin and the sweat running down its back. She was curled up with her feet under her on a davenport which seemed to contain most of the cushions in the room. She was tucked among them carefully, like a corsage in the florist's tissue paper.

She didn't turn her head. She leaned there, one hand in a small fist on her peach-colored knee. She was wearing louging pajamas of heavy ribbed silk embroidered with black lotus buds.

"You like Goodman, Miss Cressy?" Tony Reseck asked.

The girl moved her eyes slowly. The light in there was dim, but the violet of her eyes almost hurt. They were large, deep eyes without a trace of thought in them. Her face was classical and without expression.

She said nothing.

Tony smiled and moved his fingers at his sides, one by one, feeling them move. "You like Goodman, Miss Cressy?" he repeated gently.

"Not to cry over," the girl said tonelessly.

Tony rocked back on his heels and looked at her eyes. Large, deep, empty eyes. Or were they? He reached down and muted the radio.

"Don't get me wrong," the girl said. "Goodman makes money, and a lad that makes legitimate money these days is a lad you have to respect. But this jitterbug music gives me the backdrop of a beer flat. I like something with roses in it."

"Maybe you like Mozart," Tony said.

"Go on, kid me," the girl said.

"I wasn't kidding you, Miss Cressy. I think Mozart was the greatest man that ever lived—and Toscanini is his prophet."

"I thought you were the house dick." She put her head back on a pillow and stared at him through her lashes.

"Make me some of that Mozart," she added.

"It's too late," Tony sighed. "You can't get it now."

She gave him another long lucid glance. "Got the eye on me, haven't you, flatfoot?" She laughed a little, almost under her breath. "What did I do wrong?"

Tony smiled his toy smile. "Nothing, Miss Cressy. Nothing at all. But you need some fresh air. You've been five days in this hotel and you haven't been outdoors. And you have a tower room."

She laughed again. "Make me a story about it. I'm bored."

"There was a girl here once had your suite. She stayed in the hotel a whole week, like you. Without going out at all, I mean. She didn't speak to anybody hardly. What do you think she did then?"

The girl eyed him gravely. "She jumped her bill."

He put his long delicate hand out and turned it slowly, fluttering the fingers, with an effect almost like a lazy wave breaking. "Unh-uh. She sent down for her bill and paid it. Then she told the hop to be back in half an hour for her suitcases. Then she went out on her balcony."

The girl leaned forward a little, her eyes still grave, one hand capping her peach-colored knee. "What did you say your name was?"

"Tony Reseck."

"Sounds like a hunky."

"Yeah," Tony said. "Polish."

"Go on, Tony."

"All the tower suites have private balconies, Miss Cressy. The walls of them are too low for fourteen stories above the street. It was a dark night, that night, high clouds." He dropped his hand with a final gesture, a farewell gesture. "Nobody saw her jump. But when she hit, it was like a big gun going off."

"You're making it up, Tony." Her voice was a clean dry whisper of sound.

He smiled his toy smile. His quiet sea-gray eyes seemed almost to be smoothing the long waves of her hair. "Eve Cressy," he said musingly. "A name waiting for lights to be in."

"Waiting for a tall dark guy that's no good, Tony. You wouldn't care why. I was married to him once. I might be married to him again. You can make a lot of mistakes in just one lifetime." The hand on her knee opened slowly until the fingers were strained back as far as they would go. Then they closed quickly and tightly, and even in that dim light the knuckles shone like the little polished bones. "I played him a low trick once. I put him in a bad place—without meaning to. You wouldn't care about that either. It's just that I owe him something."

He leaned over softly and turned the knob on the radio. A waltz formed itself dimly on the warm air. A tinsel waltz, but a waltz. He turned the volume up. The music gushed from the loudspeaker in a swirl of shadowed melody. Since Vienna died, all waltzes are shadowed.

The girl put her hand on one side and hummed three or four bars and stopped with a sudden tightening of her mouth.

"Eve Cressy," she said. "It was in lights once. At a bum night club. A dive. They raided it and the lights went out."

He smiled at her almost mockingly. "It was no dive while you were there, Miss Cressy . . . That's the waltz the orchestra always played when the old porter walked up and down in front of the hotel entrance, all swelled up with his medals on his chest. *The Last Laugh*. Emil Jannings. You wouldn't remember that one, Miss Cressy."

" 'Spring, Beautiful Spring,' " she said. "No, I never saw it."

He walked three steps away from her and turned. "I have to go upstairs and palm doorknobs. I hope I didn't bother you. You ought to go to bed now. It's pretty late."

The tinsel waltz stopped and a voice began to talk. The girl spoke through the voice. "You really thought something like that—about the balcony?"

He nodded. "I might have," he said softly. "I don't any more."

"No chance, Tony." Her smile was a dim lost leaf. "Come and talk to me some more. Redheads don't jump, Tony. They hang on—and wither."

He looked at her gravely for a moment and then moved away over the carpet. The porter was standing in the archway that led to the main lobby. Tony hadn't looked that way yet, but he knew somebody was there. He always knew if anybody was close to him. He could hear the grass grow, like the donkey in *The Blue Bird*.

The porter jerked his chin at him urgently. His broad face above the uniform collar looked sweaty and excited. Tony stepped up close to him and they went together through the arch and out to the middle of the dim lobby.

"Trouble?" Tony asked wearily.

"There's a guy outside to see you, Tony. He won't come in. I'm doing a wipe-off on the plate glass of the doors and he comes up beside me, a tall guy. 'Get Tony,' he says, out of the side of his mouth."

Tony said: "Uh-huh," and looked at the porter's pale blue eyes. "Who was it?"

"Al, he said to say he was."

Tony's face became as expressionless as dough. "Okey." He started to move off.

The porter caught his sleeve. "Listen, Tony. You got any enemies?"

Tony laughed politely, his face still like dough.

"Listen, Tony." The porter held his sleeve tightly. "There's a big black car down the block, the other way from the hacks. There's a guy standing beside it with his foot on the running board. This guy that spoke to me, he wears a dark-colored, wrap-around overcoat with a high collar turned up against his ears. His hat's way low. You can't hardly see his face. He says, 'Get Tony,' out of the side of his mouth. You ain't got any enemies, have you, Tony?"

"Only the finance company," Tony said. "Beat it."

He walked slowly and a little stiffly across the blue carpet, up the three shallow steps to the entrance lobby with the three elevators on one side and the desk on the other. Only one elevator was working. Beside the open doors, his arms folded, the night operator stood silent in a neat blue uniform with silver facings. A lean, dark Mexican named Gomez. A new boy, breaking in on the night shift.

The other side was the desk, rose marble, with the night clerk leaning on it delicately. A small neat man with a wispy reddish mustache and cheeks so rosy they looked rouged. He stared at Tony and poked a nail at his mustache.

Tony pointed a stiff index finger at him, folded the other three fingers tight to his palm, and flicked his thumb up and down on the stiff finger. The clerk touched the other side of his mustache and looked bored.

Tony went on past the closed and darkened newsstand and the side entrance to the drugstore, out to the brassbound plate-glass doors. He stopped just inside them and took a deep, hard breath. He squared his shoulders, pushed the doors open and stepped out into the cold damp night air.

The street was dark, silent. The rumble of traffic on Wilshire, two blocks away, had no body, no meaning. To the left were two taxis. Their drivers leaned against a fender, side by side, smoking. Tony walked the other way. The big dark car was a third of a block from the hotel entrance. Its lights were dimmed and it was only when he was almost up to it that he heard the gentle sound of its engine turning over.

A tall figure detached itself from the body of the car and strolled toward him, both hands in the pockets of the dark overcoat with the high collar. From the man's mouth a cigarette tip glowed faintly, a rusty pearl.

They stopped two feet from each other.

The tall man said, "Hi, Tony. Long time no see."

"Hello, Al. How's it going?"

"Can't complain." The tall man started to take his right hand out of his overcoat pocket, then stopped and laughed quietly. "I forgot. Guess you don't want to shake hands."

"That don't mean anything," Tony said. "Shaking

hands. Monkeys can shake hands. What's on your mind, Al?"

"Still the funny little fat guy, eh, Tony?"

"I guess." Tony winked his eyes tight. His throat felt tight.

"You like your job back there?"

"It's a job."

Al laughed his quiet laugh again. "You take it slow, Tony. I'll take it fast. So it's a job and you want to hold it. Oke. There's a girl named Eve Cressy flopping in your quiet hotel. Get her out. Fast and right now."

"What's the trouble?"

The tall man looked up and down the street. A man behind in the car coughed lightly. "She's hooked with a wrong number. Nothing against her personal, but she'll lead trouble to you. Get her out, Tony. You got maybe an hour."

"Sure," Tony said aimlessly, without meaning.

Al took his hand out of his pocket and stretched it against Tony's chest. He gave him a light, lazy push. "I wouldn't be telling you just for the hell of it, little fat brother. Get her out of there."

"Okey," Tony said, without any tone in his voice.

The tall man took back his hand and reached for the car door. He opened it and started to slip in like a lean black shadow.

Then he stopped and said something to the men in the car and got out again. He came back to where Tony stood silent, his pale eyes catching a little dim light from the street.

"Listen, Tony. You always kept your nose clean. You're a good brother, Tony."

Tony didn't speak.

Al leaned toward him, a long urgent shadow, the high collar almost touching his ears. "It's trouble business, Tony. The boys won't like it, but I'm telling you just the same. This Cressy was married to a lad named Johnny Ralls. Ralls is out of Quentin two, three days, or a week. He did a three-spot for manslaughter. The girl put him there. He ran down an old man one night when he was drunk, and she was with him. He wouldn't stop. She told him to go in and tell it, or else. He didn't go in. So the Johns come for him."

Tony said, "That's too bad."

"It's kosher, kid. It's my business to know. This Ralls flapped his mouth in stir about how the girl would be waiting for him when he got out, all set to forgive and forget, and he was going straight to her."

Tony said, "What's he to you?" His voice had a dry, stiff crackle, like thick paper.

Al laughed. "The trouble boys want to see him. He ran a table at a spot on the Strip and figured out a scheme. He and another guy took the house for fifty grand. The other lad coughed up, but we still need Johnny's twenty-five. The trouble boys don't get paid to forget."

Tony looked up and down the dark street. One of the taxi drivers flicked a cigarette stub in a long arc over the top of one of the cabs. Tony watched it fall and spark on the pavement. He listened to the quiet sound of the big car's motor.

"I don't want any part of it," he said. "I'll get her out."

Al backed away from him, nodding. "Wise kid. How's mom these days?"

"Okey," Tony said.

"Tell her I was asking for her."

"Asking for her isn't anything," Tony said.

Al turned quickly and got into the car. The car curved lazily in the middle of the block and drifted back toward the corner. Its lights went up and sprayed on a wall. It turned a corner and was gone. The lingering smell of its exhaust drifted past Tony's nose. He turned and walked back to the hotel and into it. He went along to the radio room.

The radio still muttered, but the girl was gone from the davenport in front of it. The pressed cushions were hollowed out by her body. Tony reached down and touched them. He thought they were still warm. He turned the radio off and stood there, turning a thumb slowly in front of his body, his hand flat against his stomach. Then he went back through the lobby toward the elevator bank and stood beside a majolica jar of white sand. The clerk fussed behind a pebbled-glass screen at one end of the desk. The air was dead.

The elevator bank was dark. Tony looked at the indicator of the middle car and saw that it was at 14.

"Gone to bed," he said under his breath.

The door of the porter's room beside the elevators opened and the little Mexican night operator came out in street clothes. He looked at Tony with a quiet side-wise look out of eyes the color of dried-out chestnuts.

"Good night, boss."

"Yeah," Tony said absently.

He took a thin dappled cigar out of his vest pocket and smelled it. He examined it slowly, turning it around in his neat fingers. There was a small tear along the side. He frowned at that and put the cigar away.

There was a distant sound and the hand on the indicator began to steal around the bronze dial. Light glittered up in the shaft and the straight line of the car floor dissolved the darkness below. The car stopped and the doors opened, and Carl came out of it.

His eyes caught Tony's with a kind of jump and he walked over to him, his head on one side, a thin shine along his pink upper lip.

"Listen, Tony."

Tony took his arm in a hard swift hand and turned

him. He pushed him quickly, yet somehow casually, down the steps to the dim main lobby and steered him into a corner. He let go of the arm. His throat tightened again, for no reason he could think of.

"Well?" he said darkly. "Listen to what?"

The porter reached into a pocket and hauled out a dollar bill. "He gimme this," he said loosely. His glittering eyes looked past Tony's shoulder at nothing. They winked rapidly. "Ice and ginger ale."

"Don't stall," Tony growled.

"Guy in Fourteen–B," the porter said.

"Lemme smell your breath."

The porter leaned toward him obediently.

"Liquor," Tony said harshly.

"He gimme a drink."

Tony looked down at the dollar bill. "Nobody's in Fourteen–B. Not on my list," he said.

"Yeah. There is." The porter licked his lips and his eyes opened and shut several times. "Tall dark guy."

"All right," Tony said crossly. "All right. There's a tall dark guy in Fourteen–B and he gave you a buck and a drink. Then what?"

"Gat under his arm," Carl said, and blinked.

Tony smiled, but his eyes had taken on the lifeless glitter of thick ice. "You take Miss Cressy up to her room?"

Carl shook his head. "Gomez. I saw her go up."

"Get away from me," Tony said between his teeth. "And don't accept any more drinks from the guests."

He didn't move until Carl had gone back into his cubbyhole by the elevators and shut the door. Then he moved silently up the three steps and stood in front of the desk, looking at the veined rose marble, the onyx pen set, the fresh registration card in its leather frame. He lifted a hand and smacked it down hard on the marble. The clerk popped out from behind the glass screen like a chipmunk coming out of its hole.

Tony took a flimsy out of his breast pocket and spread it on the desk. "No Fourteen–B on this," he said in a bitter voice.

The clerk wisped politely at his mustache. "So sorry. You must have been out to supper when he checked in."

"Who?"

"Registered as James Watterson, San Diego." The clerk yawned.

"Ask for anybody?"

The clerk stopped in the middle of the yawn and looked at the top of Tony's head. "Why yes. He asked for a swing band. Why?"

"Smart, fast and funny," Tony said. "If you like 'em that way." He wrote on his flimsy and stuffed it back into his pocket. "I'm going upstairs and palm door-knobs. There's four tower rooms you ain't rented yet. Get up on your toes, son. You're slipping."

"I made out," the clerk drawled, and completed his yawn. "Hurry back, pop. I don't know how I'll get through the time."

"You could shave that pink fuzz off your lip," Tony said, and went across to the elevators.

He opened up a dark one and lit the dome light and shot the car up to fourteen. He darkened it again, stepped out and closed the doors. This lobby was small-er than any other, except the one immediately below it. It had a single blue-paneled door in each of the walls other than the elevator wall. On each door was a gold number and letter with a gold wreath around it. Tony walked over to 14A and put his ear to the panel. He heard nothing. Eve Cressy might be in bed asleep, or in the bathroom, or out on the balcony. Or she might be sitting there in the room, a few feet from the door,

looking at the wall. Well, he wouldn't expect to be able
to hear her sit and look at the wall. He went over to
14B and put his ear to that panel. This was different.
There was a sound in there. A man coughed. It
sounded somehow like a solitary cough. There were no
voices. Tony pressed the small nacre button beside the
door.

Steps came without hurry. A thickened voice spoke
through the panel. Tony made no answer, no sound.
The thickened voice repeated the question. Lightly,
maliciously, Tony pressed the bell again.

Mr. James Watterson, or San Diego, should now
open the door and give forth noise. He didn't. A silence
fell beyond that door that was like the silence of a
glacier. Once more Tony put his ear to the wood. Silence utterly.

He got out a master key on a chain and pushed it
delicately into the lock of the door. He turned it, pushed
the door inward three inches and withdrew the key.
Then he waited.

"All right," the voice said harshly. "Come in and
get it."

Tony pushed the door wide and stood there, framed
against the light from the lobby. The man was tall,
black-haired, angular and white-faced. He held a gun.
He held it as though he knew about guns.

"Step right in," he drawled.

Tony went in through the door and pushed it shut
with his shoulder. He kept his hands a little out from
his sides, the clever fingers curled and slack. He smiled
his quiet little smile.

"Mr. Watterson?"

"And after that what?"

"I'm the house detective here."

"It slays me."

The tall, white-faced, somehow handsome and some-

how not handsome man backed slowly into the room.
It was a large room with a low balcony around two
sides of it. French doors opened out on the little
private open-air balcony that each of the tower rooms
had. There was a grate set for a log fire behind a
paneled screen in front of a cheerful davenport. A tall
misted glass stood on a hotel tray beside a deep, cozy
chair. The man backed toward this and stood in front
of it. The large, glistening gun drooped and pointed at
the floor.

"It slays me," he said. "I'm in the dump an hour and
the house copper gives me the buzz. Okey, sweetheart,
look in the closet and bathroom. But she just left."

"You didn't see her yet," Tony said.

The man's bleached face filled with unexpected
lines. His thickened voice edged toward a snarl. "Yeah?
Who didn't I see yet?"

"A girl named Eve Cressy."

The man swallowed. He put his gun down on the
table beside the tray. He let himself down into the chair
backwards, stiffly, like a man with a touch of lumbago.
Then he leaned forward and put his hands on his knee-
caps and smiled brightly between his teeth. "So she got
here, huh? I didn't ask about her yet. I'm a careful
guy. I didn't ask yet."

"She's been here five days," Tony said. "Waiting for
you. She hasn't left the hotel a minute."

The man's mouth worked a little. His smile had a
knowing tilt to it. "I got delayed a little up north," he
said smoothly. "You know how it is. Visiting old
friends. You seem to know a lot about my business,
copper."

"That's right, Mr. Ralls."

The man lunged to his feet and his hand snapped at
the gun. He stood leaning over, holding it on the table,
staring. "Dames talk too much," he said with a muffled

sound in his voice as though he held something soft between his teeth and talked through it.

"Not dames, Mr. Ralls."

"Huh?" The gun slithered on the hard wood of the table. "Talk it up, copper. My mind reader just quit."

"Not dames, guys. Guys with guns."

The glacier silence fell between them again. The man straightened his body out slowly. His face was washed clean of expression, but his eyes were haunted. Tony leaned in front of him, a shortish plump man with a quiet, pale, friendly face and eyes as simple as forest water.

"They never run out of gas—those boys," Johnny Ralls said, and licked at his lip. "Early and late, they work. The old firm never sleeps."

"You know who they are?" Tony said softly.

"I could maybe give nine guesses. And twelve of them would be right."

"The trouble boys," Tony said, and smiled a brittle smile.

"Where is she?" Johnny Ralls asked harshly.

"Right next door to you."

The man walked to the wall and left his gun lying on the table. He stood in front of the wall, studying it. He reached up and gripped the grillwork of the balcony railing. When he dropped his hand and turned, his face had lost some of its lines. His eyes had a quieter glint. He moved back to Tony and stood over him.

"I've got a stake," he said. "Eve sent me some dough and I built it up with a touch I made up north. Case dough, what I mean. The trouble boys talk about twenty-five grand." He smiled crookedly. "Five *C's* I can count. I'd have a lot of fun making them believe that, I would."

"What did you do with it?" Tony asked indifferently.

"I never had it, copper. Leave that lay. I'm the only

guy in the world that believes it. It was a little deal that I got suckered on."

"I'll believe it," Tony said.

"They don't kill often. But they can be awful tough."

"Mugs," Tony said with a sudden bitter contempt. "Guys with guns. Just mugs."

Johnny Ralls reached for his glass and drained it empty. The ice cubes tinkled softly as he put it down. He picked his gun up, danced it on his palm, then tucked it, nose down, into an inner breast pocket. He stared at the carpet.

"How come you're telling me this, copper?"

"I thought maybe you'd give her a break."

"And if I wouldn't?"

"I kind of think you will," Tony said.

Johnny Ralls nodded quietly. "Can I get out of here?"

"You could take the service elevator to the garage. You could rent a car. I can give you a card to the garage man."

"You're a funny little guy," Johnny Ralls said.

Tony took out a worn ostrich-skin billfold and scribbled on a printed card. Johnny Ralls read it, and stood holding it, tapping it against a thumbnail.

"I could take her with me," he said, his eyes narrow.

"You could take a ride in a basket too," Tony said. "She's been here five days, I told you. She's been spotted. A guy I know called me up and told me to get her out of here. Told me what it was all about. So I'm getting you out instead."

"They'll love that," Johnny Ralls said. "They'll send you violets."

"I'll weep about it on my day off."

Johnny Ralls turned his hand over and stared at the

palm. "I could see her, anyway. Before I blow. Next door to here, you said?"

Tony turned on his heel and started for the door. He said over his shoulder, "Don't waste a lot of time, handsome. I might change my mind."

The man said, almost gently: "You might be spotting me right now, for all I know."

Tony didn't turn his head. "That's a chance you have to take."

He went on to the door and passed out of the room. He shut it carefully, silently, looked once at the door of 14A and got into his dark elevator. He rode it down to the linen-room floor and got out to remove the basket that held the service elevator open at that floor. The door slid quietly shut. He held it so that it made no noise. Down the corridor, light came from the open door of the housekeeper's office. Tony got back into his elevator and went on down to the lobby.

The little clerk was out of sight behind his pebbled-glass screen, auditing accounts. Tony went through the main lobby and turned into the radio room. The radio was on again, soft. She was there, curled on the davenport again. The speaker hummed to her, a vague sound so low that what it said was as wordless as the murmur of trees. She turned her head slowly and smiled at him.

"Finished palming doorknobs? I couldn't sleep worth a nickel. So I came down again. Okey?"

He smiled and nodded. He sat down in a green chair and patted the plump brocade arms of it. "Sure, Miss Cressy."

"Waiting is the hardest kind of work, isn't it? I wish you'd talk to that radio. It sounds like a pretzel being bent."

Tony fiddled with it, got nothing he liked, set it back where it had been.

"Beer-parlor drunks are all the customers now."

She smiled at him again.

"I don't bother you being here, Miss Cressy?"

"I like it. You're a sweet little guy, Tony."

He looked stiffly at the floor and a ripple touched his spine. He waited for it to go away. It went slowly. Then he sat back, relaxed again, his neat fingers clasped on his elk's tooth. He listened. Not to the radio—to far-off, uncertain things, menacing things. And perhaps to just the safe whir of wheels going away into a strange night.

"Nobody's all bad," he said out loud.

The girl looked at him lazily. "I've met two or three I was wrong on, then."

He nodded. "Yeah," he admitted judiciously. "I guess there's some that are."

The girl yawned and her deep violet eyes half closed. She nestled back into the cushions. "Sit there for a while, Tony. Maybe I could nap."

"Sure. Not a thing for me to do. Don't know why they pay me."

She slept quickly and with complete stillness, like a child. Tony hardly breathed for ten minutes. He just watched her, his mouth a little open. There was a quiet fascination in his limpid eyes, as if he was looking at an altar.

Then he stood up with infinite care and padded away under the arch to the entrance lobby and the desk. He stood at the desk listening for a little while. He heard a pen rustling out of sight. He went around the corner to the row of house phones in little glass cubbyholes. He lifted one and asked the night operator for the garage.

It rang three or four times and then a boyish voice answered: "Windermere Hotel. Garage speaking."

"This is Tony Reseck. That guy Watterson I gave a card to. He leave?"

"Sure, Tony. Half an hour almost. Is it your charge?"

"Yeah," Tony said. "My party. Thanks. Be seein' you."

He hung up and scratched his neck. He went back to the desk and slapped a hand on it. The clerk wafted himself around the screen with his greeter's smile in place. It dropped when he saw Tony.

"Can't a guy catch up on his work?" he grumbled.

"What's the professional rate on Fourteen–B?"

The clerk stared morosely. "There's no professional rate in the tower."

"Make one. The fellow left already. Was there only an hour."

"Well, well," the clerk said airily. "So the personality didn't click tonight. We get a skip-out."

"Will five bucks satisfy you?"

"Friend of yours?"

"No. Just a drunk with delusions of grandeur and no dough."

"Guess we'll have to let it ride, Tony. How did he get out?"

"I took him down the service elevator. You was asleep. Will five bucks satisfy you?"

"Why?"

The worn ostrich-skin wallet came out and a weedy five slipped across the marble. "All I could shake him for," Tony said loosely.

The clerk took the five and looked puzzled. "You're the boss," he said, and shrugged. The phone shrilled on the desk and he reached for it. He listened and then pushed it toward Tony. "For you."

Tony took the phone and cuddled it close to his chest. He put his mouth close to the transmitter. The voice was strange to him. It had a metallic sound. Its syllables were meticulously anonymous.

"Tony? Tony Reseck?"

"Talking."

"A message from Al. Shoot?"

Tony looked at the clerk. "Be a pal," he said over the mouthpiece. The clerk flicked a narrow smile at him and went away. "Shoot," Tony said into the phone.

"We had a little business with a guy in your place. Picked him up scramming. Al had a hunch you'd run him out. Tailed him and took him to the curb. Not so good. Backfire."

Tony held the phone very tight and his temples chilled with the evaporation of moisture. "Go on," he said. "I guess there's more."

"A little. The guy stopped the big one. Cold. Al—Al said to tell you goodbye."

Tony leaned hard against the desk. His mouth made a sound that was not speech.

"Get it?" The metallic voice sounded impatient, a little bored. "This guy had him a rod. He used it. Al won't be phoning anybody any more."

Tony lurched at the phone, and the base of it shook on the rose marble. His mouth was a hard dry knot.

The voice said: "That's as far as we go, bub. G'night." The phone clicked dryly, like a pebble hitting a wall.

Tony put the phone down in its cradle very carefully, so as not to make any sound. He looked at the clenched palm of his left hand. He took a handkerchief out and rubbed the palm softly and straightened the fingers out with his other hand. Then he wiped his forehead. The clerk came around the screen again and looked at him with glinting eyes.

"I'm off Friday. How about lending me that phone number?"

Tony nodded at the clerk and smiled a minute frail smile. He put his handkerchief away and patted the pocket he had put it in. He turned and walked away from the desk, across the entrance lobby, down the three shallow steps, along the shadowy reaches of the main lobby, and so in through the arch to the radio room once more. He walked softly, like man moving in a room where somebody is very sick. He reached the chair he had sat in before and lowered himself into it inch by inch. The girl slept on, motionless, in that curled-up looseness achieved by some women and all cats. Her breath made no slightest sound against the vague murmur of the radio.

Tony Reseck leaned back in the chair and clasped his hands on his elk's tooth and quietly closed his eyes.

# THE KING IN YELLOW

GEORGE MILLAR, night auditor at the Carlton Hotel, was a dapper wiry little man, with a soft deep voice like a torch singer's. He kept it low, but his eyes were sharp and angry, as he said into the PBX mouthpiece: "I'm very sorry. It won't happen again. I'll send up at once."

He tore off the headpiece, dropped it on the keys of the switchboard and marched swiftly from behind the pebbled screen and out into the entrance lobby. It was past one and the Carlton was two-thirds residential. In the main lobby, down three shallow steps, lamps were dimmed and the night porter had finished tidying up. The place was deserted—a wide space of dim furniture, rich carpet. Faintly in the distance a radio sounded. Millar went down the steps and walked quickly towards the sound, turned through an archway and looked at a man stretched out on a pale green davenport and what looked like all the loose cushions in the hotel. He lay on his side dreamy-eyed and listened to the radio two yards away from him.

Millar barked: "Hey, you! Are you the house dick here or the house cat?"

Steve Grayce turned his head slowly and looked at Millar. He was a long black-haired man, about twenty-eight, with deep-set silent eyes and a rather gentle mouth. He jerked a thumb at the radio and smiled. "King Leopardi, George. Hear that trumpet tone. Smooth as an angel's wing, boy."

"Swell! Go on back upstairs and get him out of the corridor!"

Steve Grayce looked shocked. "What—again? I thought I had those birds put to bed long ago." He swung his feet to the floor and stood up. He was at least a foot taller than Millar.

"Well, Eight-sixteen says no. Eight-sixteen says he's out in the hall with two of his stooges. He's dressed in yellow satin shorts and a trombone and he and his pals are putting on a jam session. And one of those hustlers Quillan registered in Eight-eleven is out there truckin' for them. Now get on to it, Steve—and this time make it stick."

Steve Grayce smiled wryly. He said: "Leopardi doesn't belong here anyway. Can I use chloroform or just my blackjack?"

He stepped long legs over the pale-green carpet, through the arch and across the main lobby to the single elevator that was open and lighted. He slid the doors shut and ran it up to Eight, stopped it roughly and stepped out into the corridor.

The noise hit him like a sudden wind. The walls echoed with it. Half a dozen doors were open and angry guests in night robes stood in them peering.

"It's O.K. folks," Steve Grayce said rapidly. "This is absolutely the last act. Just relax."

He rounded a corner and the hot music almost took him off his feet. Three men were lined up against the wall, near an open door from which light streamed. The middle one, the one with the trombone, was six feet tall, powerful and graceful, with a hairline mustache. His face was flushed and his eyes had an alcoholic glitter. He wore yellow satin shorts with large initials embroidered in black on the left leg—nothing more. His torso was tanned and naked.

The two with him were in pajamas, the usual half-way-good-looking band boys, both drunk, but not staggering drunk. One jittered madly on a clarinet and the other on a tenor saxophone.

Back and forth in front of them, strutting, trucking, preening herself like a magpie, arching her arms and her eyebrows, bending her fingers back until the carmine nails almost touched her arms, a metallic blonde swayed and went to town on the music. Her voice was a throaty screech, without melody, as false as her eyebrows and as sharp as her nails. She wore high-heeled slippers and black pajamas with a long purple sash.

Steve Grayce stopped dead and made a sharp downward motion with his hand. "Wrap it up!" he snapped. "Can it. Put it on ice. Take it away and bury it. The show's out. Scram, now—scram!"

King Leopardi took the trombone from his lips and bellowed: "Fanfare to a house dick!"

The three drunks blew a stuttering note that shook the walls. The girl laughed foolishly and kicked out. Her slipper caught Steve Grayce in the chest. He picked it out of the air, jumped towards the girl and took hold of her wrist.

"Tough, eh?" he grinned. "I'll take you first."

"Get him!" Leopardi yelled. "Sock him low! Dance the gum-heel on his neck!"

Steve swept the girl off her feet, tucked her under his arm and ran. He carried her as easily as a parcel. She tried to kick his legs. He laughed and shot a glance through a lighted doorway. A man's brown brogues lay under a bureau. He went on past that to a second lighted doorway, slammed through and kicked the door shut, turned far enough to twist the tabbed key in the lock. Almost at once a fist hit the door. He paid no attention to it.

He pushed the girl along the short passage past the bathroom, and let her go. She reeled away from him and put her back to the bureau, panting, her eyes furious. A lock of damp gold-dipped hair swung down over one eye. She shook her head violently and bared her teeth.

"How would you like to get vagged, sister?"

"Go to hell!" she spit out. "The King's a friend of mine, see? You better keep your paws off me, copper."

"You run the circuit with the boys?"

She spat at him again.

"How'd you know they'd be here?"

Another girl was sprawled across the bed, her head to the wall, tousled black hair over a white face. There was a tear in the leg of her pajamas. She lay limp and groaned.

Steve said harshly: "Oh, oh, the torn-pajama act. It flops here, sister, it flops hard. Now listen, you kids. You can go to bed and stay till morning or you can take the bounce. Make up your minds."

The black-haired girl groaned. The blonde said: "You get out of my room, you damned gum-heel!"

She reached behind her and threw a hand mirror. Steve ducked. The mirror slammed against the wall and fell without breaking. The black-haired girl rolled over on the bed and said wearily: "Oh lay off. I'm sick."

She lay with her eyes closed, the lids fluttering.

The blonde swiveled her hips across the room to a desk by the window, poured herself a full half-glass of Scotch in a water glass and gurgled it down before

Steve could get to her. She choked violently, dropped the glass and went down on her hands and knees.

Steve said grimly: "That's the one that kicks you in the face, sister."

The girl crouched, shaking her head. She gagged once, lifted the carmine nails to paw at her mouth. She tried to get up, and her foot skidded out from under her and she fell down on her side and went fast asleep.

Steve sighed, went over and shut the window and fastened it. He rolled the black-haired girl over and straightened her on the bed and got the bedclothes from under her, tucked a pillow under her head. He picked the blonde bodily off the floor and dumped her on the bed and covered both girls to the chin. He opened the transom, switched off the ceiling light and unlocked the door. He relocked it from the outside, with a master key on a chain.

"Hotel business," he said under his breath. "Phooey."

The corridor was empty now. One lighted door still stood open. Its number was 815, two doors from the room the girls were in. Trombone music came from it softly—but not softly enough for 1.25 A.M.

Steve Grayce turned into the room, crowded the door shut with his shoulder and went along past the bathroom. King Leopardi was alone in the room.

The bandleader was sprawled out in an easy chair, with a tall misted glass at his elbow. He swung the trombone in a tight circle as he played it and the lights danced in the horn.

Steve lit a cigarette, blew a plume of smoke and stared through it at Leopardi with a queer, half-admiring, half-contemptuous expression.

He said softly: "Lights out, yellow-pants. You play a sweet trumpet and your trombone don't hurt either.

But we can't use it here. I already told you that once. Lay off. Put that thing away."

Leopardi smiled nastily and blew a stuttering raspberry that sounded like a devil laughing.

"Says you," he sneered. "Leopardi does what he likes, where he likes, when he likes. Nobody's stopped him yet, gum-shoe. Take the air."

Steve hunched his shoulders and went close to the tall dark man. He said patiently: "Put that bazooka down, big-stuff. People are trying to sleep. They're funny that way. You're a great guy on a band shell. Everywhere else you're just a guy with a lot of jack and a personal reputation that stinks from here to Miami and back. I've got a job to do and I'm doing it. Blow that thing again and I'll wrap it around your neck."

Leopardi lowered the trombone and took a long drink from the glass at his elbow. His eyes glinted nastily. He lifted the trombone to his lips again, filled his lungs with air and blew a blast that rocked the walls. Then he stood up very suddenly and smoothly and smashed the instrument down on Steve's head.

"I never did like house peepers," he sneered. "They smell like public toilets."

Steve took a short step back and shook his head. He leered, slid forward on one foot and smacked Leopardi open-handed. The blow looked light, but Leopardi reeled all the way across the room and sprawled at the foot of the bed, sitting on the floor, his right arm draped in an open suitcase.

For a moment neither man moved. Then Steve kicked the trombone away from him and squashed his cigarette in a glass tray. His black eyes were empty but his mouth grinned whitely.

"If you want trouble," he said, "I come from where they make it."

Leopardi smiled, thinly, tautly, and his right hand came up out of the suitcase with a gun in it. His thumb snicked the safety catch. He held the gun steady, pointing.

"Make some with this," he said, and fired.

The bitter roar of the gun seemed a tremendous sound in the closed room. The bureau mirror splintered and glass flew. A sliver cut Steve's cheek like a razor blade. Blood oozed in a small narrow line on his skin.

He left his feet in a dive. His right shoulder crushed against Leopardi's bare chest and his left hand brushed the gun away from him, under the bed. He rolled swiftly to his right and came up on his knees spinning.

He said thickly, harshly: "You picked the wrong gee, brother."

He swarmed on Leopardi and dragged him to his feet by his hair, by main strength. Leopardi yelled and hit him twice on the jaw and Steve grinned and kept his left hand twisted in the bandleader's long sleek black hair. He turned his hand and the head twisted with it and Leopardi's third punch landed on Steve's shoulder. Steve took hold of the wrist behind the punch and twisted that and the bandleader went down on his knees yowling. Steve lifted him by the hair again, let go of his wrist and punched him three times in the stomach, short terrific jabs. He let go of the hair then as he sank the fourth punch almost to his wrist.

Leopardi sagged blindly to his knees and vomited.

Steve stepped away from him and went into the bathroom and got a towel off the rack. He threw it at Leopardi, jerked the open suitcase onto the bed and started throwing things into it.

Leopardi wiped his face and got to his feet still gagging. He swayed, braced himself on the end of the bureau. He was white as a sheet.

Steve Grayce said: "Get dressed, Leopardi. Or go out the way you are. It's all one to me.

Leopardi stumbled into the bathroom, pawing the wall like a blind man.

# 2

Millar stood very still behind the desk as the elevator opened. His face was white and scared and his cropped black mustache was a smudge across his upper lip. Leopardi came out of the elevator first, a muffler around his neck, a lightweight coat tossed over his arm, a hat tilted on his head. He walked stiffly, bent forward a little, his eyes vacant. His face had a greenish pallor.

Steve Grayce stepped out behind him carrying a suitcase, and Carl, the night porter, came last with two more suitcases and two instrument cases in black leather. Steve marched over to the desk and said harshly: "Mr. Leopardi's bill—if any. He's checking out."

Millar goggled at him across the marble desk. "I—I don't think, Steve—"

"O.K. I thought not."

Leopardi smiled very thinly and unpleasantly and walked out through the brass-edged swing doors the porter held open for him. There were two nighthawk cabs in the line. One of them came to life and pulled up to the canopy and the porter loaded Leopardi's stuff into it. Leopardi got into the cab and leaned forward to put his head to the open window. He said slowly and thickly: "I'm sorry for you, gum-heel. I mean sorry."

Steve Grayce stepped back and looked at him woodenly. The cab moved off down the street, rounded a corner and was gone. Steve turned on his heel, took a

quarter from his pocket and tossed it up in the air. He
slapped it into the night porter's hand.

"From the King," he said. "Keep it to show your
grandchildren."

He went back into the hotel, got into the elevator
without looking at Millar, shot it up to Eight again and
went along the corridor, master-keyed his way into
Leopardi's room. He relocked it from the inside, pulled
the bed out from the wall and went in behind it. He
got a .32 automatic off the carpet, put it in his pocket
and prowled the floor with his eyes looking for the
ejected shell. He found it against the wastebasket,
reached to pick it up, and stayed bent over, staring
into the basket. His mouth tightened. He picked up the
shell and dropped it absently into his pocket, then
reached a questing finger into the basket and lifted out
a torn scrap of paper on which a piece of newsprint
had been pasted. Then he picked up the basket, pushed
the bed back against the wall and dumped the con-
tents of the basket out on it.

From the trash of torn papers and matches he sep-
arated a number of pieces with newsprint pasted to
them. He went over to the desk with them and sat
down. A few minutes later he had the torn scraps put
together like a jigsaw puzzle and could read the message that had been made by cutting words and letters
from magazines and pasting them on a sheet.

TEN GRand BY TH U RS DAY  NI GHT,
LEO PAR DI. DAY AFTER *YOU* OPEN AT
T HE CL U B SHAL OTTE.  OR EL SE—CUR-
TAINS.  FROM HER BROTHER.

Steve Grayce said: "Huh." He scooped the torn
pieces into a hotel envelope, put that in his inside breast
pocket and lit a cigarette. "The guy had guts," he said.
"I'll grant him that—and his trumpet."

He locked the room, listened a moment in the now silent corridor, then went along to the room occupied by the two girls. He knocked softly and put his ear to the panel. A chair squeaked and feet came towards the door.

"What is it?" The girl's voice was cool, wide awake. It was not the blonde's voice.

"The house man. Can I speak to you a minute?"

"You're speaking to me."

"Without the door between, lady."

"You've got the passkey. Help yourself." The steps went away. He unlocked the door with his master key, stepped quietly inside, and shut it. There was a dim light in a lamp with a shirred shade on the desk. On the bed the blonde snored heavily, one hand clutched in her brilliant metallic hair. The black-haired girl sat in the chair by the window, her legs crossed at right angles like a man's and stared at Steve emptily.

He went close to her and pointed to the long tear in her pajama leg. He said softly: "You're not sick. You were not drunk. That tear was done a long time ago. What's the racket? A shakedown on the King?"

The girl stared at him coolly, puffed at a cigarette and said nothing.

"He checked out," Steve said. "Nothing doing in that direction now, sister." He watched her like a hawk, his black eyes hard and steady on her face.

"Aw, you house dicks make me sick!" the girl said with sudden anger. She surged to her feet and went past him into the bathroom, shut and locked the door.

Steve shrugged and felt the pulse of the girl asleep in the bed—a thumpy, draggy pulse, a liquor pulse.

"Poor damn hustlers," he said under his breath.

He looked at a large purple bag that lay on the bureau, lifted it idly and let it fall. His face stiffened again. The bag made a heavy sound on the glass top, as if there were a lump of lead inside it. He snapped it open quickly and plunged a hand in. His fingers touched the cold metal of a gun. He opened the bag wide and stared down into it at a small .25 automatic. A scrap of white paper caught his eye. He fished it out and held it to the light—a rent receipt with a name and address. He stuffed it into his pocket, closed the bag and was standing by the window when the girl came out of the bathroom.

"Hell, are you still haunting me?" she snapped. "You know what happens to hotel dicks that master-key their way into ladies' bedrooms at night?"

Steve said loosely: "Yeah. They get in trouble. They might even get shot at."

The girl's face became set, but her eyes crawled sideways and looked at the purple bag. Steve looked at her. "Know Leopardi in Frisco?" he asked. "He hasn't played here in two years. Then he was just a trumpet player in Vane Utigore's band—a cheap outfit."

The girl curled her lip, went past him and sat down by the window again. Her face was white, stiff. She said dully: "Blossom did. That's Blossom on the bed."

"Know he was coming to this hotel tonight?"

"What makes it your business?"

"I can't figure him coming here at all," Steve said. "This is a quiet place. So I can't figure anybody coming here to put the bite on him."

"Go somewhere else and figure. I need sleep."

Steve said: "Good night, sweetheart—and keep your door locked."

A thin man with thin blond hair and thin face was standing by the desk, tapping on the marble with thin fingers. Millar was still behind the desk and he still looked white and scared. The thin man wore a dark gray suit with a scarf inside the collar of the coat. He had a look of having just got up. He turned sea-green eyes slowly on Steve as he got out of the elevator, waited for him to come up to the desk and throw a tabbed key on it.

Steve said: "Leopardi's key, George. There's a busted mirror in his room and the carpet has his dinner on it—mostly Scotch." He turned to the thin man. "You want to see me, Mr. Peters?"

"What happened, Grayce?" The thin man had a tight voice that expected to be lied to.

"Leopardi and two of his boys were on Eight, the rest of the gang on Five. The bunch on Five went to bed. A couple of obvious hustlers managed to get themselves registered just two rooms from Leopardi. They managed to contact him and everybody was having a lot of nice noisy fun out in the hall. I could only stop it by getting a little tough."

"There's blood on your cheek," Peters said coldly. "Wipe it off."

Steve scratched at his cheek with a handkerchief. The thin thread of blood had dried. "I got the girls tucked away in their room," he said. "The two stooges took the hint and holed up, but Leopardi still thought the guests wanted to hear trombone music. I threatened to wrap it around his neck and he beaned me with it. I slapped him open-handed and he pulled a gun and took a shot at me. Here's the gun."

He took the .32 automatic out of his pocket and laid it on the desk. He put the used shell beside it. "So I beat some sense into him and threw him out," he added.

Peters tapped on the marble. "Your usual tact seems to have been well in evidence."

Steve stared at him. "He shot at me," he repeated quietly. "With a gun. This gun. I'm tender to bullets.

He missed, but suppose he hadn't? I like my stomach the way it is, with just one way in and one way out."

Peters narrowed his tawny eyebrows. He said very politely: "We have you down on the payroll here as a night clerk, because we don't like the name house detective. But neither night clerks nor house detectives put guests out of the hotel without consulting me. Not ever, Mr. Grayce."

Steve said: "The guy shot at me, pal. With a gun. Catch on? I don't have to take that without a kick-back, do I?" His face was a little white.

Peters said: "Another point for your consideration. The controlling interest in this hotel is owned by Mr. Halsey G. Walters. Mr. Walters also owns the Club Shalotte, where King Leopardi is opening on Wednesday night. And that, Mr. Grayce, is why Leopardi was good enough to give us his business. Can you think of anything else I should like to say to you?"

"Yeah. I'm canned," Steve said mirthlessly.

"Very correct, Mr. Grayce. Good-night, Mr. Grayce."

The thin blond man moved to the elevator and the night porter took him up.

Steve looked at Millar.

"Jumbo Walters, huh?" he said softly. "A tough, smart guy. Much too smart to think this dump and the Club Shalotte belong to the same sort of customers. Did Peters write Leopardi to come here?"

"I guess he did, Steve." Millar's voice was low and gloomy.

"Then why wasn't he put in a tower suite with a private balcony to dance on, at twenty-eight bucks a day? Why was he put on a medium-priced transient floor? And why did Quillan let those girls get so close to him?"

Millar pulled at his black mustache. "Tight with

money—as well as with Scotch, I suppose. As to the girls, I don't know."

Steve slapped the counter open-handed. "Well, I'm canned, for not letting a drunken heel make a parlor house and a shooting gallery out of the eighth floor. Nuts! Well, I'll miss the joint at that."

"I'll miss you too, Steve," Millar said gently. "But not for a week. I take a week off starting tomorrow. My brother has a cabin at Crestline."

"Didn't know you had a brother," Steve said absently. He opened and closed his fist on the marble desk top.

"He doesn't come into town much. A big guy. Used to be a fighter."

Steve nodded and straightened from the counter. "Well, I might as well finish out the night," he said. "On my back. Put this gun away somewhere, George."

He grinned coldly and walked away, down the steps into the dim main lobby and across to the room where the radio was. He punched the pillows into shape on the pale green davenport, then suddenly reached into his pocket and took out the scrap of white paper he had lifted from the black-haired girl's purple handbag. It was a receipt for a week's rent, to a Miss Marilyn Delorme, Apt. 211, Ridgeland Apartments, 118 Court Street.

He tucked it into his wallet and stood staring at the silent radio. "Steve, I think you got another job," he said under his breath. "Something about this set-up smells."

He slipped into a closetlike phone booth in the corner of the room, dropped a nickel and dialed an all-night radio station. He had to dial four times before he got a clear line to the Owl Program announcer.

"How's to play King Leopardi's record of 'Solitude' again?" he asked him.

"Got a lot of requests piled up. Played it twice already. Who's calling?"

"Steve Grayce, night man at the Carlton Hotel."

"Oh, a sober guy on his job. For you, pal, anything."

Steve went back to the davenport, snapped the radio on and lay down on his back, with his hands clasped behind his head.

Ten minutes later the high, piercingly sweet trumpet notes of King Leopardi came softly from the radio, muted almost to a whisper, and sustaining E above high C for an almost incredible period of time.

"Shucks," Steve grumbled, when the record ended. "A guy that can play like that—maybe I was too tough with him."

## 3

Court Street was old town, wop town, crook town, arty town. It lay across the top of Bunker Hill and you could find anything there from down-at-heels ex-Greenwich-villagers to crooks on the lam, from ladies of anybody's evening to County Relief clients brawling with haggard landladies in grand old houses with scrolled porches, parquetry floors, and immense sweeping banisters of white oak, mahogany and Circassian walnut.

It had been a nice place once, had Bunker Hill, and from the days of its niceness there still remained the funny little funicular railway, called the Angel's Flight, which crawled up and down a yellow clay bank from Hill Street. It was afternoon when Steve Grayce got off the car at the top, its only passenger. He walked along in the sun, a tall, wide-shouldered, rangy-looking man in a well-cut blue suit.

He turned west at Court and began to read the numbers. The one he wanted was two from the corner, across the street from a red brick funeral parlor with a sign in gold over it: Paolo Perrugini Funeral Home. A swarthy iron-gray Italian in a cutaway coat stood in front of the curtained door of the red brick building, smoking a cigar and waiting for somebody to die.

One-eighteen was a three-storied frame apartment house. It had a glass door, well masked by a dirty net curtain, a hall runner eighteen inches wide, dim doors with numbers painted on them with dim paint, a staircase halfway back. Brass stair rods glittered in the dimness of the hallway.

Steve Grayce went up the stairs and prowled back to the front. Apartment 211, Miss Marilyn Delorme, was on the right, a front apartment. He tapped lightly on the wood, waited, tapped again. Nothing moved beyond the silent door, or in the hallway. Behind another door across the hall somebody coughed and kept on coughing.

Standing there in the half-light Steve Grayce wondered why he had come. Miss Delorme had carried a gun. Leopardi had received some kind of a threat letter and torn it up and thrown it away. Miss Delorme had checked out of the Carlton about an hour after Steve told her Leopardi was gone. Even at that—

He took out a leather keyholder and studied the lock of the door. It looked as if it would listen to reason. He tried a pick on it, snicked the bolt back and stepped softly into the room. He shut the door, but the pick wouldn't lock it.

The room was dim with drawn shades across two front windows. The air smelled of face powder. There was light-painted furniture, a pull-down double bed which was pulled down but had been made up. There was a magazine on it, a glass tray full of cigarette butts, a pint bottle half full of whiskey, and a glass on a chair

beside the bed. Two pillows had been used for a back
rest and were still crushed in the middle.

On the dresser there was a composition toilet set,
neither cheap nor expensive, a comb with black hair in
it, a tray of manicuring stuff, plenty of spilled powder
—in the bathroom, nothing. In a closet behind the bed
a lot of clothes and two suitcases. The shoes were all
one size.

Steve stood beside the bed and pinched his chin.
"Blossom, the spitting blonde, doesn't live here," he
said under his breath. "Just Marilyn the torn-pants
brunette."

He went back to the dresser and pulled drawers out.
In the bottom drawer, under the piece of wall paper
that lined it, he found a box of .25 copper-nickel automatic shells. He poked at the butts in the ash tray. All
had lipstick on them. He pinched his chin again, then
feathered the air with the palm of his hand, like an
oarsman with a scull.

"Bunk," he said softly. "Wasting your time, Stevie."

He walked over to the door and reached for the knob,
then turned back to the bed and lifted it by the foot-
rail.

Miss Marilyn Delorme was in.

She lay on her side on the floor under the bed, long
legs scissored out as if in running. One mule was on,
one off. Garters and skin showed at the tops of her
stockings, and a blue rose on something pink. She wore
a square-necked, short-sleeved dress that was not too
clean. Her neck above the dress was blotched with purple bruises.

Her face was a dark plum color, her eyes had the
faint stale glitter of death, and her mouth was open so
far that it foreshortened her face. She was colder than
ice, and still quite limp. She had been dead two or
three hours at least, six hours at most.

The purple bag was beside her, gaping like her mouth. Steve didn't touch any of the stuff that had been emptied out on the floor. There was no gun and there were no papers.

He let the bed down over her again, then made the rounds of the apartment, wiping everything he had touched and a lot of things he couldn't remember whether he had touched or not.

He listened at the door and stepped out. The hall was still empty. The man behind the opposite door still coughed. Steve went down the stairs, looked at the mailboxes and went back along the lower hall to a door.

Behind this door a chair creaked monotonously. He knocked and a woman's sharp voice called out. Steve opened the door with his handkerchief and stepped in.

In the middle of the room a woman rocked in an old Boston rocker, her body in the slack boneless attitude of exhaustion. She had a mud-colored face, stringy hair, gray cotton stockings—everything a Bunker Hill landlady should have. She looked at Steve with the interested eye of a dead goldfish.

"Are you the manager?"

The woman stopped rocking, screamed, "Hi, Jake! Company!" at the top of her voice, and started rocking again.

An icebox door thudded shut behind a partly open inner door and a very big man came into the room carrying a can of beer. He had a doughy mooncalf face, a tuft of fuzz on top of an otherwise bald head, a thick brutal neck and chin, and brown pig eyes about as expressionless as the woman's. He needed a shave—had needed one the day before—and his collarless shirt gaped over a big hard hairy chest. He wore scarlet suspenders with large gilt buckles on them.

He held the can of beer out to the woman. She

clawed it out of his hand and said bitterly: "I'm so tired I ain't got no sense."

The man said: "Yah. You ain't done the halls so good at that."

The woman snarled: "I done 'em as good as I aim to." She sucked the beer thirstily.

Steve looked at the man and said: "Manager?"

"Yah. 'S me. Jake Stoyanoff. Two hun'erd eighty-six stripped, and still plenty tough."

Steve said: "Who lives in Two-eleven?"

The big man leaned forward a little from the waist and snapped his suspenders. Nothing changed in his eyes. The skin along his big jaw may have tightened a little. "A dame," he said.

"Alone?"

"Go on—ask me," the big man said. He stuck his hand out and lifted a cigar off the edge of a stained-wood table. The cigar was burning unevenly and it smelled as if somebody had set fire to the doormat. He pushed it into his mouth with a hard, thrusting motion, as if he expected his mouth wouldn't want it to go in.

"I'm asking you," Steve said.

"Ask me out in the kitchen," the big man drawled.

He turned and held the door open. Steve went past him.

The big man kicked the door shut against the squeak of the rocking chair, opened up the icebox and got out two cans of beer. He opened them and handed one to Steve.

"Dick?"

Steve drank some of the beer, put the can down on the sink, got a brand-new card out of his wallet—a business card printed that morning. He handed it to the man.

The man read it, put it down on the sink, picked it

up and read it again. "One of them guys," he growled over his beer. "What's she pulled this time?"

Steve shrugged and said: "I guess it's the usual. The torn-pajama act. Only there's a kickback this time."

"How come? You handling it, huh? Must be a nice cozy one."

Steve nodded. The big man blew smoke from his mouth. "Go ahead and handle it," he said.

"You don't mind a pinch here?"

The big man laughed heartily. "Nuts to you, brother," he said pleasantly enough. "You're a private dick. So it's a hush. O.K. Go out and hush it. And if it *was* a pinch—that bothers me like a quart of milk. Go into your act. Take all the room you want. Cops don't bother Jake Stoyanoff."

Steve stared at the man. He didn't say anything. The big man talked it up some more, seemed to get more interested. "Besides," he went on, making motions with the cigar, "I'm softhearted. I never turn up a dame. I never put a frill in the middle." He finished his beer and threw the can in a basket under the sink, and pushed his hand out in front of him, revolving the large thumb slowly against the next two fingers. "Unless there's some of that," he added.

Steve said softly: "You've got big hands. You could have done it."

"Huh?" His small brown leathery eyes got silent and stared.

Steve said: "Yeah. You might be clean. But with those hands the cops'd go round and round with you just the same."

The big man moved a little to his left, away from the sink. He let his right hand hang down at his side, loosely. His mouth got so tight that the cigar almost touched his nose.

"What's the beef, huh?" he barked. "What you shovin' at me, guy? What—"

"Cut it," Steve drawled. "She's been croaked. Strangled. Upstairs, on the floor under her bed. About midmorning, I'd say. Big hands did it—hands like yours."

The big man did a nice job of getting the gun off his hip. It arrived so suddenly that it seemed to have grown in his hand and been there all the time.

Steve frowned at the gun and didn't move. The big man looked him over. "You're tough," he said. "I been in the ring long enough to size up a guy's meat. You're plenty hard, boy. But you ain't as hard as lead. Talk it up fast."

"I knocked at her door. No answer. The lock was a pushover. I went in. I almost missed her because the bed was pulled down and she had been sitting on it, reading a magazine. There was no sign of struggle. I lifted the bed just before I left—and there she was. Very dead, Mr. Stoyanoff. Put the gat away. Cops don't bother you, you said a minute ago."

The big man whispered: "Yes and no. They don't make me happy neither. I get a bump once'n a while. Mostly a Dutch. You said something about my hands, mister."

Steve shook his head. "That was a gag," he said. "Her neck has nail marks. You bite your nails down close. You're clean."

The big man didn't look at his fingers. He was very pale. There was sweat on his lower lips, in the black stubble of his beard. He was still leaning forward, still motionless, when there was a knocking beyond the kitchen door, the door from the living room to the hall-way. The creaking chair stopped and the woman's sharp voice screamed: "Hi, Jake! Company!"

The big man cocked his head. "That old slut

wouldn't climb off'n her fanny if the house caught fire," he said thickly.

He stepped to the door and slipped through it, locking it behind him.

Steve ranged the kitchen swiftly with his eyes. There was a small high window beyond the sink, a trap low down for a garbage pail and parcels, but no other door. He reached for his card Stoyanoff had left lying on the drainboard and slipped it back into his pocket. Then he took a short-barreled Detective Special out of his left breast pocket where he wore it nose down, as in a holster.

He had got that far when the shots roared beyond the wall—muffled a little, but still loud—four of them blended in a blast of sound.

Steve stepped back and hit the kitchen door with his leg out straight. It held and jarred him to the top of his head and in his hip joint. He swore, took the whole width of the kitchen and slammed into it with his left shoulder. It gave this time. He pitched into the living room. The mud-faced woman sat leaning forward in her rocker, her head to one side and a lock of mousy hair smeared down over her bony forehead.

"Backfire, huh?" she said stupidly. "Sounded kinda close. Musta been in the alley."

Steve jumped across the room, yanked the outer door open and plunged out into the hall.

The big man was still on his feet, a dozen feet down the hallway, in the direction of a screen door that opened flush on an alley. He was clawing at the wall. His gun lay at his feet. His left knee buckled and he went down on it.

A door was flung open and a hard-looking woman peered out, and instantly slammed her door shut again. A radio suddenly gained in volume beyond her door.

The big man got up off his left knee and the leg

shook violently inside his trousers. He went down on both knees and got the gun into his hand and began to crawl towards the screen door. Then, suddenly he went down flat on his face and tried to crawl that way, grinding his face into the narrow hall runner.

Then he stopped crawling and stopped moving altogether. His body went limp and the hand holding the gun opened and the gun rolled out of it.

Steve hit the screen door and was out in the alley. A gray sedan was speeding towards the far end of it. He stopped, steadied himself and brought his gun up level, and the sedan whisked out of sight around the corner.

A man boiled out of another apartment house across the alley. Steve ran on, gesticulating back at him and pointing ahead. As he ran he slipped the gun back into his pocket. When he reached the end of the alley, the gray sedan was out of sight. Steve skidded around the wall onto the sidewalk, slowed to a walk and then stopped.

Half a block down a man finished parking a car, got out and went across the sidewalk to a lunchroom. Steve watched him go in, then straightened his hat and walked along the wall to the lunchroom.

He went in, sat at the counter and ordered coffee. In a little while there were sirens.

Steve drank his coffee, asked for another cup and drank that. He lit a cigarette and walked down the long hill to Fifth, across to Hill, back to the foot of the Angel's Flight, and got his convertible out of a parking lot.

He drove out west, beyond Vermont, to the small hotel where he had taken a room that morning.

# 4

Bill Dockery, floor manager of the Club Shalotte, teetered on his heels and yawned in the unlighted entrance to the dining room. It was a dead hour for business, late cocktail time, too early for dinner, and much too early for the real business of the club, which was high-class gambling.

Dockery was a handsome mug in a midnight-blue dinner jacket and a maroon carnation. He had a two-inch forehead under black lacquer hair, good features a little on the heavy side, alert brown eyes and very long curly eyelashes which he liked to let down over his eyes, to fool troublesome drunks into taking a swing at him.

The entrance door of the foyer was opened by the uniformed doorman and Steve Grayce came in.

Dockery said, "Ho, hum," tapped his teeth and leaned his weight forward. He walked across the lobby slowly to meet the guest. Steve stood just inside the doors and ranged his eyes over the high foyer walled with milky glass, lighted softly from behind. Molded in the glass were etchings of sailing ships, beasts of the jungle, Siamese pagodas, temples of Yucatan. The doors were square frames of chromium, like photo frames. The Club Shalotte had all the class there was, and the mutter of voices from the bar lounge on the left was not noisy. The faint Spanish music behind the voices was delicate as a carved fan.

Dockery came up and leaned his sleek head forward an inch. "May I help you?"

"King Leopardi around?"

Dockery leaned back again. He looked less interested. "The bandleader? He opens tomorrow night."

"I thought he might be around—rehearsing or something."

"Friend of his?"

"I know him. I'm not job-hunting, and I'm not a song plugger if that's what you mean."

Dockery teetered on his heels. He was tone-deaf and Leopardi meant no more to him than a bag of peanuts. He half smiled. "He was in the bar lounge a while ago." He pointed with his square rock-like chin. Steve Grayce went into the bar lounge.

It was about a third full, warm and comfortable and not too dark nor too light. The little Spanish orchestra was in an archway, playing with muted strings small seductive melodies that were more like memories than sounds. There was no dance floor. There was a long bar with comfortable seats, and there were small round composition-top tables, not too close together. A wall seat ran around three sides of the room. Waiters flitted among the tables like moths.

Steve Grayce saw Leopardi in the far corner, with a girl. There was an empty table on each side of him. The girl was a knockout.

She looked tall and her hair was the color of a brush fire seen through a dust cloud. On it, at the ultimate rakish angle, she wore a black velvet double-pointed beret with two artificial butterflies made of polka-dotted feathers and fastened on with tall silver pins. Her dress was burgundy-red wool and the blue fox draped over one shoulder was at least two feet wide. Her eyes were large, smoke-blue, and looked bored. She slowly turned a small glass on the table top with a gloved left hand.

Leopardi faced her, leaning forward, talking. His shoulders looked very big in a shaggy, cream-colored sports coat. Above the neck of it his hair made a point on his brown neck. He laughed across the table as

Steve came up, and his laugh had a confidant, sneering sound.

Steve stopped, then moved behind the next table. The movement caught Leopardi's eye. His head turned, he looked annoyed, and then his eyes got very wide and brilliant and his whole body turned slowly, like a mechanical toy.

Leopardi put both his rather small well-shaped hands down on the table, on either side of a highball glass. He smiled. Then he pushed his chair back and stood up. He put one finger up and touched his hairline mustache, with theatrical delicacy. Then he said drawlingly, but distinctly: "You son of a bitch!"

A man at a nearby table turned his head and scowled. A waiter who had started to come over stopped in his tracks, then faded back among the tables. The girl looked at Steve Grayce and then leaned back against the cushions of the wall seat and moistened the end of one bare finger on her right hand and smoothed a chestnut eyebrow.

Steve stood quite still. There was a sudden high flush on his cheekbones. He said softly: "You left something at the hotel last night. I think you ought to do something about it. Here."

He reached a folded paper out of his pocket and held it out. Leopardi took it, still smiling, opened it and read it. It was a sheet of yellow paper with torn pieces of white paper pasted on it. Leopardi crumpled the sheet and let it drop at his feet.

He took a smooth step towards Steve and repeated more loudly: "You son of a bitch!"

The man who had first looked around stood up sharply and turned. He said clearly: "I don't like that sort of language in front of my wife."

Without even looking at the man Leopardi said: "To hell with you and your wife."

The man's face got a dusky red. The woman with him stood up and grabbed a bag and a coat and walked away. After a moment's indecision the man followed her. Everybody in the place was staring now. The waiter who had faded back among the tables went through the doorway into the entrance foyer, walking very quickly.

Leopardi took another, longer step and slammed Steve Grayce on the jaw. Steve rolled with the punch and stepped back and put his hand down on another table and upset a glass. He turned to apologize to the couple at the table. Leopardi jumped forward very fast and hit him behind the ear.

Dockery came through the doorway, split two waiters like a banana skin and started down the room showing all his teeth.

Steve gagged a little and ducked away. He turned and said thickly: "Wait a minute, you fool—that isn't all of it—there's——"

Leopardi closed in fast and smashed him full on the mouth. Blood oozed from Steve's lip and crawled down the line at the corner of his mouth and glistened on his chin. The girl with the red hair reached for her bag, white-faced with anger, and started to get up from behind her table.

Leopardi turned abruptly on his heel and walked away. Dockery put out a hand to stop him. Leopardi brushed it aside and went on, went out of the lounge.

The tall red-haired girl put her bag down on the table again and dropped her handkerchief on the floor. She looked at Steve quietly, spoke quietly. "Wipe the blood off your chin before it drips on your shirt." She had a soft, husky voice with a trill in it.

Dockery came up harsh-faced, took Steve by the arm and put weight on the arm. "All right, you! Let's go!"

Steve stood quite still, his feet planted, staring at the

girl. He dabbed at his mouth with a handkerchief. He half smiled. Dockery couldn't move him an inch. Dockery dropped his hand, signaled two waiters and they jumped behind Steve, but didn't touch him.

Steve felt his lip carefully and looked at the blood on his handkerchief. He turned to the people at the table behind him and said: "I'm terribly sorry. I lost my balance."

The girl whose drink he had spilled was mopping her dress with a small fringed napkin. She smiled up at him and said: "It wasn't your fault."

The two waiters suddenly grabbed Steve's arms from behind. Dockery shook his head and they let go again. Dockery said tightly: "You hit him?"

"No."

"You say anything to make him hit you?"

"No."

The girl at the corner table bent down to get her fallen handkerchief. It took her quite a time. She finally got it and slid into the corner behind the table again. She spoke coldly.

"Quite right, Bill. It was just some more of the King's sweet way with his public."

Dockery said "Huh?" and swiveled his head on his thick hard neck. Then he grinned and looked back at Steve.

Steve said grimly: "He gave me three good punches, one from behind, without a return. You look pretty hard. See can you do it."

Dockery measured him with his eyes. He said evenly: "You win. I couldn't . . . Beat it!" he added sharply to the waiters. They went away. Dockery sniffed his carnation, and said quietly: "We don't go for brawls in here." He smiled at the girl again and went away, saying a word here and there at the tables. He went out through the foyer doors.

Steve tapped his lip, put his handkerchief in his pocket and stood searching the floor with his eyes.

The red-haired girl said calmly: "I think I have what you want—in my handkerchief. Won't you sit down?"

Her voice had a remembered quality, as if he had heard it before.

He sat down opposite her, in the chair where Leopardi had been sitting.

The red-haired girl said: "The drink's on me. I was with him."

Steve said, "Coke with a dash of bitters," to the waiter.

The waiter said: "Madame?"

"Brandy and soda. Light on the brandy, please." The waiter bowed and drifted away. The girl said amusedly: "Coke with a dash of bitters. That's what I love about Hollywood. You meet so many neurotics."

Steve stared into her eyes and said softly: "I'm an occasional drinker, the kind of guy who goes out for a beer and wakes up in Singapore with a full beard."

"I don't believe a word of it. Have you know the King long?"

"I met him last night. I didn't get along with him."

"I sort of noticed that." She laughed. She had a rich low laugh, too.

"Give me that paper, lady."

"Oh, one of these impatient men. Plenty of time." The handkerchief with the crumpled yellow sheet inside it was clasped tightly in her gloved hand. Her middle right finger played with an eyebrow. "You're not in pictures, are you?"

"Hell, no."

"Same here. Me, I'm too tall. The beautiful men have to wear stilts in order to clasp me to their bosoms."

The waiter set the drinks down in front of them,

made a grace note in the air with his napkin and went away.

Steve said quietly, stubbornly: "Give me that paper, lady."

"I don't like that 'lady' stuff. It sounds like cop to me."

"I don't know your name."

"I don't know yours. Where did you meet Leopardi?"

Steve sighed. The music from the little Spanish orchestra had a melancholy minor sound now and the muffled clicking of gourds dominated it.

Steve listened to it with is head on one side. He said: "The E string is a half-tone flat. Rather cute effect."

The girl stared at him with new interest. "I'd never have noticed that," she said. "And I'm supposed to be a pretty good singer. But you haven't answered my question."

He said slowly: "Last night I was house dick at the Carlton Hotel. They called me night clerk, but house dick was what I was. Leopardi stayed there and cut up too rough. I threw him out and got canned."

The girl said: "Ah. I begin to get the idea. He was being the King and you were being—if I might guess— a pretty tough order of house detective."

"Something like that. Now will you please—"

"You still haven't told me your name."

He reached for his wallet, took one of the brand-new cards out of it and passed it across the table. He sipped his drink while she read it.

"A nice name," she said slowly. "But not a very good address. And *Private investigator* is bad. It should have been *Investigations,* very small, in the lower left-hand corner."

"They'll be small enough," Steve grinned. "Now will you please—"

She reached suddenly across the table and dropped the crumpled ball of paper in his hand.

"Of course I haven't read it—and of course I'd like to. You do give me that much credit, I hope"—she looked at the card again, and added—"Steve. Yes, and your office should be in a Georgian or very modernistic building in the Sunset Eighties. Suite Something-or-other. And your clothes should be very jazzy. Very jazzy indeed, Steve. To be inconspicuous in this town is to be a busted flush."

He grinned at her. His deep-set black eyes had lights in them. She put the card away in her bag, gave her fur piece a yank, and drank about half of her drink. "I have to go." She signaled the waiter and paid the check. The waiter went away and she stood up.

Steve said sharply: "Sit down."

She stared at him wonderingly. Then she sat down again and leaned against the wall, still staring at him. Steve leaned across the table, asked "How well do *you* know Leopardi?"

"Off and on for years. If it's any of your business. Don't go masterful on me, for God's sake. I loathe masterful men. I once sang for him, but not for long. You can't just sing for Leopardi—if you get what I mean."

"You were having a drink with him."

She nodded slightly and shrugged. "He opens here tomorrow night. He was trying to talk me into singing for him again. I said no, but I may have to, for a week or two anyway. The man who owns the Club Shalotte also owns my contract—and the radio station where I work a good deal."

"Jumbo Walters," Steve said. "They say he's tough

but square. I never met him, but I'd like to. After all I've got a living to get. Here."

He reached back across the table and dropped the crumpled paper. "The name was—"

"Dolores Chiozza."

Steve repeated it lingeringly. "I like it. I like your singing too. I've heard a lot of it. You don't oversell a song, like most of these high-money torchers." His eyes glistened.

The girl spread the paper on the table and read it slowly, without expression. Then she said quietly: "Who tore it up?"

"Leopardi, I guess. The pieces were in his wastebasket last night. I put them together, after he was gone. The guy has guts—or else he gets these things so often they don't register any more."

"Or else he thought it was a gag." She looked across the table levelly, then folded the paper and handed it back.

"Maybe. But if he's the kind of guy I hear he is— one of them is going to be on the level and the guy behind it is going to do more than just shake him down."

Dolores Chiozza said: "He's the kind of guy you hear he is."

"It wouldn't be hard for a woman to get to him then —would it—a woman with a gun?"

She went on staring at him. "No. And everybody would give her a big hand, if you ask me. If I were you, I'd just forget the whole thing. If he wants protection—Walters can throw more around him than the police. If he doesn't—who cares? I don't. I'm damn sure I don't."

"You're kind of tough yourself, Miss Chiozza—over some things."

She said nothing. Her face was a little white and more than a little hard.

Steve finished his drink, pushed his chair back and reached for his hat. He stood up. "Thank you very much for the drink, Miss Chiozza. Now that I've met you I'll look forward all the more to hearing you sing again."

"You're damn formal all of a sudden," she said.

He grinned. "So long, Dolores."

"So long, Steve. Good luck—in the sleuth racket. If I hear of anything—"

He turned and walked among the tables out of the bar lounge.

## 5

In the crisp fall evening the lights of Hollywood and Los Angeles winked at him. Searchlight beams probed the cloudless sky as if searching for bombing-planes.

Steve got his convertible out of the parking lot and drove it east along Sunset. At Sunset and Fairfax he bought an evening paper and pulled over to the curb to look through it. There was nothing in the paper about 118 Court Street.

He drove on and ate dinner at the little coffee shop beside his hotel and went to a movie. When he came out he bought a Home Edition of the *Tribune,* a morning sheet. They were in that—both of them.

Police thought Jake Stoyanoff might have strangled the girl, but she had not been attacked. She was described as a stenographer, unemployed at the moment. There was no picture of her. There was a picture of Stoyanoff that looked like a touched-up police photo. Police were looking for a man who had been talking to Stoyanoff just before he was shot. Several people said he was a tall man in a dark suit. That was all the description the police got—or gave out.

Steve grinned sourly, stopped at the coffee shop for a good-night cup of coffee and then went up to his room. It was a few minutes to eleven o'clock. As he unlocked his door the telephone started to ring.

He shut the door and stood in the darkness remembering where the phone was. Then he walked straight to it, catlike in the dark room, sat in an easy chair and reached the phone up from the lower shelf of a small table. He held the one-piece to his ear and said: "Hello."

"Is this Steve?" It was a rich, husky voice, low, vibrant. It held a note of strain.

"Yeah, this is Steve. I can hear you. I know who you are."

There was a faint dry laugh. "You'll make a detective after all. And it seems I'm to give you your first case. Will you come over to my place at once? It's Twenty-four-twelve Renfrew—North, there isn't any South—just half a block below Fountain. It's a sort of bungalow court. My house is the last in line, at the back."

Steve said: "Yes. Sure. What's the matter?"

There was a pause. A horn blared in the street outside the hotel. A wave of white light went across the ceiling from some car rounding the corner uphill. The low voice said very slowly: "Leopardi. I can't get rid of him. He's—he's passed out in my bedroom." Then a tinny laugh that didn't go with the voice at all.

Steve held the phone so tight his hand ached. His teeth clicked in the darkness. He said flatly, in a dull, brittle voice: "Yeah. It'll cost you twenty bucks."

"Of course. Hurry, please."

He hung up, sat there in the dark room breathing hard. He pushed his hat back on his head, then yanked it forward again with a vicious jerk and laughed out loud. "Hell," he said, *"That* kind of a dame."

Twenty-four-twelve Renfrew was not strictly a bungalow court. It was a staggered row of six bungalows, all facing the same way, but so-arranged that no two of their front entrances overlooked each other. There was a brick wall at the back and beyond the brick wall a church. There was a long smooth lawn, moon-silvered.

The door was up two steps, with lanterns on each side and an iron-work grill over the peep hole. This opened to his knock and a girl's face looked out, a small oval face with a Cupid's-bow mouth, arched and plucked eyebrows, wavy brown hair. The eyes were like two fresh and shiny chestnuts.

Steve dropped a cigarette and put his foot on it. "Miss Chiozza. She's expecting me. Steve Grayce."

"Miss Chiozza has retired, sir," the girl said with a half-insolent twist to her lips.

"Break it up, kid. You heard me, I'm expected."

The wicket slammed shut. He waited, scowling back along the narrow moonlit lawn towards the street. O.K. So it was like that—well, twenty bucks was worth a ride in the moonlight anyway.

The lock clicked and the door opened wide. Steve went past the maid into a warm cheerful room, old-fashioned with chintz. The lamps were neither old nor new and there were enough of them—in the right places. There was a hearth behind a paneled copper screen, a davenport close to it, a bar-top radio in the corner.

The maid said stiffly: "I'm sorry, sir. Miss Chiozza forgot to tell me. Please have a chair." The voice was soft, and it might be cagey. The girl went off down the room—short skirts, sheer silk stockings, and four-inch spike heels.

Steve sat down and held his hat on his knee and scowled at the wall. A swing door creaked shut. He got a cigarette out and rolled it between his fingers and then deliberately squeezed it to a shapeless flatness of white paper and ragged tobacco. He threw it away from him, at the fire screen.

Dolores Chiozza came towards him. She wore green velvet lounging pajamas with a long gold-fringed sash. She spun the end of the sash as if she might be going to throw a loop with it. She smiled a slight artificial smile. Her face had a clean scrubbed look and her eyelids were bluish and they twitched.

Steve stood up and watched the green morocco slippers peep out under the pajamas as she walked. When she was close to him he lifted his eyes to her face and said dully: "Hello."

She looked at him very steadily, then spoke in a nigh, carrying voice. "I know it's late, but I knew you were used to being up all night. So I thought what we had to talk over— Won't you sit down?"

She turned her head very slightly, seemed to be listening for something.

Steve said: "I never go to bed before two. Quite all right."

She went over and pushed a bell beside the hearth. After a moment the maid came through the arch.

"Bring some ice cubes, Agatha. Then go along home. It's getting pretty late."

"Yes'm." The girl disappeared.

There was a silence then that almost howled till the tall girl took a cigarette absently out of a box, put it between her lips and Steve struck a match clumsily on his shoe. She pushed the end of the cigarette into the flame and her smoke-blue eyes were very steady on his black ones. She shook her head very slightly.

The maid came back with a copper ice bucket. She

pulled a low Indian-brass tray-table between them before the davenport, put the ice bucket on it, then a
siphon, glasses and spoons, and a triangular bottle that
looked like good Scotch had come in it except that it
was covered with silver filigree work and fitted with a
stopper.

Dolores Chiozza said, "Will you mix a drink?" in a
formal voice.

He mixed two drinks, stirred them, handed her one.
She sipped it, shook her head. "Too light," she said. He
put more whiskey in it and handed it back. She said,
"Better," and leaned back against the corner of the
davenport.

The maid came into the room again. She had a small
rakish red hat on her wavy brown hair and was wearing a gray coat trimmed with nice fur. She carried a
black brocade bag that could have cleaned out a fair-
sized icebox. She said: "Good night, Miss Dolores."

"Good night, Agatha."

The girl went out the front door, closed it softly. Her
heels clicked down the walk. A car door opened and
shut distantly and a motor started. Its sound soon
dwindled away. It was a very quiet neighborhood.

Steve put his drink down on the brass tray and
looked levelly at the tall girl, said harshly: "That means
she's out of the way?"

"Yes. She goes home in her own car. She drives me
home from the studio in mine—when I go to the studio,
which I did tonight. I don't like to drive a car myself."

"Well, what are you waiting for?"

The red-haired girl looked steadily at the paneled
fire screen and the unlit log fire behind it. A muscle
twitched in her cheek.

After a moment she said: "Funny that I called you
instead of Walters. He'd have protected me better than
you can. Only he wouldn't have believed me. I thought

perhaps you would. I didn't invite Leopardi here. So far as I know—we two are the only people in the world who know he's here."

Something in her voice jerked Steve upright.

She took a small crisp handkerchief from the breast pocket of the green velvet pajama-suit, dropped it on the floor, picked it up swiftly and pressed it against her mouth. Suddenly, without making a sound, she began to shake like a leaf.

Steve said swiftly: "What the hell—I can handle that heel in my hip pocket. I did last night—and last night he had a gun and took a shot at me."

Her head turned. Her eyes were very wide and staring. "But it couldn't have been my gun," she said in a dead voice.

"Huh? Of course not—what—?"

"It's my gun tonight," she said and stared at him. "You said a woman could get to him with a gun very easily."

He just stared at her. His face was white now and he made a vague sound in his throat.

"He's not drunk, Steve," she said gently. "He's dead. In yellow pajamas—in my bed. With my gun in his hand. You didn't think he was just drunk—did you, Steve?"

He stood up in a swift lunge, then became absolutely motionless, staring down at her. He moved his tongue on his lips and after a long time he formed words with it. "Let's go look at him," he said in a hushed voice.

# 6

The room was at the back of the house to the left. The girl took a key out of her pocket and unlocked the door. There was a low light on a table, and the venetian blinds were drawn. Steve went in past her silently, on cat feet.

Leopardi lay squarely in the middle of the bed, a large smooth silent man, waxy and artificial in death. Even his mustache looked phony. His half-open eyes, sightless as marbles, looked as if they had never seen. He lay on his back, on the sheet, and the bedclothes were thrown over the foot of the bed.

The King wore yellow silk pajamas, the slip-on kind, with a turned collar. They were loose and thin. Over his breast they were dark with blood that had seeped into the silk as if into blotting-paper. There was a little blood on his bare brown neck.

Steve stared at him and said tonelessly: "The King in Yellow. I read a book with that title once. He liked yellow, I guess. I packed some of his stuff last night. And he wasn't yellow either. Guys like him usually are—or are they?"

The girl went over to the corner and sat down in a slipper chair and looked at the floor. It was a nice room, as modernistic as the living room was casual. It had a chenille rug, café-au-lait color, severely angled furniture in inlaid wood, and a trick dresser with a mirror for a top, a kneehole and drawers like a desk. It had a box mirror above and a semi-cylindrical frosted wall light set above the mirror. In the corner there was a glass table with a crystal greyhound on top of it, and a lamp with the deepest drum shade Steve had ever seen.

He stopped looking at all this and looked at Leopardi again. He pulled the King's pajamas up gently and examined the wound. It was directly over the heart and the skin was scorched and mottled there. There was not so very much blood. He had died in a fraction of a second.

A small Mauser automatic lay cuddled in his right hand, on top of the bed's second pillow.

"That's artistic," Steve said and pointed. "Yeah, that's a nice touch. Typical contact wound, I guess. He even pulled his pajama shirt up. I've heard they do that. A Mauser seven-six-three about. Sure it's your gun?"

"Yes." She kept on looking at the floor. "It was in a desk in the living room—not loaded. But there were shells. I don't know why. Somebody gave it to me once. I didn't even know how to load it."

Steve smiled. Her eyes lifted suddenly and she saw his smile and shuddered. "I don't expect anybody to believe that," she said. "We may as well call the police, I suppose."

Steve nodded absently, put a cigarette in his mouth and flipped it up and down with his lips that were still puffy from Leopardi's punch. He lit a match on his thumbnail, puffed a small plume of smoke and said quietly: "No cops. Not yet. Just tell it."

The red-haired girl said: "I sing at KFQC, you know. Three nights a week—on a quarter-hour automobile program. This was one of the nights. Agatha and I got home—oh, close to half-past ten. At the door I remembered there was no fizzwater in the house, so I sent her back to the liquor store three blocks away, and came in alone. There was a queer smell in the house. I don't know what it was. As if several men had been in here, somehow. When I came in the bedroom—he was exactly as he is now. I saw the gun and I went and looked and then I knew I was sunk. I didn't know what to do. Even if the police cleared me, everywhere I went from now on—"

Steve said sharply: "He got in here—how?"

"I don't know."

"Go on," he said.

"I locked the door. Then I undressed—with that on

my bed. I went into the bathroom to shower and collect my brains, if any. I locked the door when I left the room and took the key. Agatha was back then, but I don't think she saw me. Well, I took the shower and it braced me up a bit. Then I had a drink and then I came in here and called you."

She stopped and moistened the end of a finger and smoothed the end of her left eyebrow with it. "That's all, Steve—absolutely all."

"Domestic help can be pretty nosy. This Agatha's noiser than most—or I miss my guess." He walked over to the door and looked at the lock. "I bet there are three or four keys in the house that knock this over." He went to the windows and felt the catches, looked down at the screens through the glass. He said over his shoulder, casually: "Was the King in love with you?"

Her voice was sharp, almost angry. "He never was in love with any woman. A couple of years back in San Francisco, when I was with his band for a while, there was some slap-silly publicity about us. Nothing to it. It's been revived here in the hand-outs to the press, to build up his opening. I was telling him this afternoon I wouldn't stand for it, that I wouldn't be linked with him in anybody's mind. His private life was filthy. It reeked. Everybody in the business knows that. And it's not a business where daisies grow very often."

Steve said: "Yours was the only bedroom he couldn't make?"

The girl flushed to the roots of her dusky red hair.

"That sounds lousy," he said. "But I have to figure the angles. That's about true, isn't it?"

"Yes—I suppose so. I wouldn't say the only one."

"Go on out in the other room and buy yourself a drink."

She stood up and looked at him squarely across the

bed. "I didn't kill him, Steve. I didn't let him into this house tonight. I didn't know he was coming here, or had any reason to come here. Believe that or not. But something about this is wrong. Leopardi was the last man in the world to take his lovely life himself."

Steve said: "He didn't, angel. Go buy that drink. He was murdered. The whole thing is a frame——to get a cover-up from Jumbo Walters. Go on out."

He stood silent, motionless, until sounds he heard from the living room told him she was out there. Then he took out his handkerchief and loosened the gun from Leopardi's right hand and wiped it over carefully on the outside, broke out the magazine and wiped that off, spilled out all the shells and wiped every one, ejected the one in the breech and wiped that. He reloaded the gun and put it back in Leopardi's dead hand and closed his fingers around it and pushed his index finger against the trigger. Then he let the hand fall naturally back on the bed.

He pawed through the bedclothes and found an ejected shell and wiped that off, put it back where he had found it. He put the handkerchief to his nose, sniffed it wryly, went around the bed to a clothes closet and opened the door.

"Careless of your clothes, boy," he said softly.

The rough cream-colored coat hung in there, on a hook, over dark gray slacks with a lizard-skin belt. A yellow satin shirt and a wine-colored tie dangled alongside. A handkerchief to match the tie flowed loosely four inches from the breast pocket of the coat. On the floor lay a pair of gazelle-leather nutmeg-brown sports shoes, and socks without garters. And there were yellow satin shorts with heavy black initials on them lying close by.

Steve felt carefully in the gray slacks and got out a leather keyholder. He left the room, went along the cross-hall and into the kitchen. It had a solid door, a good spring lock with a key stuck in it. He took it out and tried keys from the bunch in the keyholder, found none that fitted, put the other key back and went into the living room. He opened the front door, went outside and shut it again without looking at the girl huddled in a corner of the davenport. He tried keys in the lock, finally found the right one. He let himself back into the house, returned to the bedroom and put the keyholder back in the pocket of the gray slacks again. Then he went to the living room.

The girl was still huddled motionless, staring at him.

He put his back to the mantel and puffed at a cigarette. "Agatha with you all the time at the studio?"

She nodded. "I suppose so. So he had a key. That was what you were doing, wasn't it?"

"Yes. Had Agatha long?"

"About a year."

"She steal from you? Small stuff, I mean?"

Dolores Chiozza shrugged wearily. "What does it matter? Most of them do. A little face cream or powder, a handkerchief, a pair of stockings once in a while. Yes, I think she stole from me. They look on that sort of thing as more or less legitimate."

"Not the nice ones, angel."

"Well—the hours were a little trying. I work at night, often get home very late. She's a dresser as well as a maid."

"Anything else about her? She use cocaine or weed. Hit the bottle? Ever have laughing fits?"

"I don't think so. What has she got to do with it, Steve?"

"Lady, she sold somebody a key to your apartment. That's obvious. You didn't give him one, the landlord wouldn't give him one, but Agatha had one. Check?"

Her eyes had a stricken look. Her mouth trembled

a little, not much. A drink was untasted at her elbow. Steve bent over and drank some of it.

She said slowly: "We're wasting time, Steve. We have to call the police. There's nothing anybody can do. I'm done for as a nice person, even if not as a lady at large. They'll think it was a lovers' quarrel and I shot him and that's that. If I could convince them I didn't, then he shot himself in my bed, and I'm still ruined. So I might as well make up my mind to face the music."

Steve said softly: "Watch this. My mother used to do it."

He put a finger to his mouth, bent down and touched her lips at the same spot with the same finger. He smiled, said: "We'll go to Walters—or you will. He'll pick his cops and the ones he picks won't go screaming through the night with reporters sitting in their laps. They'll sneak in quiet, like process servers. Walters can handle this. That was what was counted on. Me, I'm going to collect Agatha. Because I want a description of the guy she sold that key to—and I want it fast. And by the way, you owe me twenty bucks for coming over here. Don't let that slip your memory."

The tall girl stood up, smiling. "You're a kick, you are," she said. "What makes you so sure he was murdered?"

"He's not wearing his own pajamas. His have his initials on them. I packed his stuff last night—before I threw him out of the Carlton. Get dressed, angel—and get me Agatha's address."

He went into the bedroom and pulled a sheet over Leopardi's body, held it a moment above the still, waxen face before letting it fall.

"So long, guy," he said gently. "You were a louse— but you sure had music in you."

It was a small frame house on Brighton Avenue near Jefferson, in a block of small frame houses, all old-fashioned, with front porches. This one had a narrow concrete walk which the moon made whiter than it was.

Steve mounted the steps and looked at the light-edged shade of the wide front window. He knocked. There were shuffling steps and a woman opened the door and looked at him through the hooked screen—a dumpy elderly woman with frizzled gray hair. Her body was shapeless in a wrapper and her feet slithered in loose slippers. A man with a polished bald head and milky eyes sat in a wicker chair beside a table. He held his hands in his lap and twisted the knuckles aimlessly. He didn't look towards the door.

Steve said: "I'm from Miss Chiozza. Are you Agatha's mother?"

The woman said dully: "I reckon. But she ain't home, mister." The man in the chair got a handkerchief from somewhere and blew his nose. He snickered darkly.

Steve said: "Miss Chiozza's not feeling so well tonight. She was hoping Agatha would come back and stay the night with her."

The milky-eyed man snickered again, sharply. The woman said: "We dunno where she is. She don't come home. Pa'n me waits up for her to come home. She stays out till we're sick."

The old man snapped in a reedy voice: "She'll stay out till the cops get her one of these times."

"Pa's half blind," the woman said. "Makes him kinda mean. Won't you step in?"

Steve shook his head and turned his hat around in his hands like a bashful cowpuncher in a horse opera. "I've got to find her," he said. "Where would she go?"

"Out drinkin' liquor with cheap spenders," Pa

cackled. "Panty-waists with silk handkerchiefs 'stead of neckties. If I had eyes, I'd strap her till she dropped." He grabbed the arms of his chair and the muscles knotted on the backs of his hands. Then he began to cry. Tears welled from his milky eyes and started through the white stubble on his cheeks. The woman went across and took the handkerchief out of his fist and wiped his face with it. Then she blew her nose on it and came back to the door.

"Might be anywhere," she said to Steve. "This is a big town, mister. I dunno where at to say."

Steve said dully: "I'll call back. If she comes in, will you hang onto her. What's your phone number?"

"What's the phone number, Pa?" the woman called back over her shoulder."

"I ain't sayin'," Pa snorted.

The woman said: "I remember now. South Two-four-five-four. Call any time. Pa'n me ain't got nothing to do."

Steve thanked her and went back down the white walk to the street and along the walk half a block to where he had left his car. He glanced idly across the way and started to get into his car, then stopped moving suddenly with his hand gripping the car door. He let go of that, took three steps sideways and stood looking across the street tight-mouthed.

All the houses in the block were much the same, but the one opposite had a FOR RENT placard stuck in the front window and a real-estate sign spiked into the small patch of front lawn. The house itself looked neglected, utterly empty, but in its little driveway stood a small neat black coupe.

Steve said under his breath: "Hunch. Play it up, Stevie."

He walked almost delicately across the wide dusty street, his hand touching the hard metal of the gun in his pocket, and came up behind the little car, stood and listened. He moved silently along its left side, glanced back across the street, then looked in the car's open left-front window.

The girl sat almost as if driving, except that her head was tipped a little too much into the corner. The little red hat was still on her head, the gray coat, trimmed with fur, still around her body. In the reflected moonlight her mouth was strained open. Her tongue stuck out. And her chestnut eyes stared at the roof of the car.

Steve didn't touch her. He didn't have to touch her to look any closer to know there would be heavy bruises on her neck.

"Tough on women, these guys," he muttered.

The girl's big black brocade bag lay on the seat beside her, gaping open like her mouth—like Miss Marilyn Delorme's mouth, and Miss Marilyn Delorme's purple bag.

"Yeah—tough on women."

He backed away till he stood under a small palm tree by the entrance to the driveway. The street was as empty and deserted as a closed theater. He crossed silently to his car, got into it and drove away.

Nothing to it. A girl coming home alone late at night, stuck up and strangled a few doors from her own home by some tough guy. Very simple. The first prowl car that cruised that block—if the boys were half awake —would take a look the minute they spotted the FOR RENT sign. Steve tramped hard on the throttle and went away from there.

At Washington and Figueroa he went into an all-night drugstore and pulled shut the door of the phone booth at the back. He dropped his nickel and dialed the number of police headquarters.

He asked for the desk and said: "Write this down, will you, sergeant? Brighton Avenue, thirty-two-hundred block, west side, in driveway of empty house. Got that much?"

"Yeah. So what?"

"Car with dead woman in it," Steve said, and hung up.

# 7

Quillan, head day clerk and assistant manager of the Carlton Hotel, was on night duty, because Millar, the night auditor, was off for a week. It was half-past one and things were dead and Quillan was bored. He had done everything there was to do long ago, because he had been a hotel man for twenty years and there was nothing to it.

The night porter had finished cleaning up and was in his room beside the elevator bank. One elevator was lighted and open, as usual. The main lobby had been tidied up and the lights had been properly dimmed. Everything was exactly as usual.

Quillan was a rather short, rather thickset man with clear bright toadlike eyes that seemed to hold a friendly expression without really having any expression at all. He had pale sandy hair and not much of it. His pale hands were clasped in front of him on the marble top of the desk. He was just the right height to put his weight on the desk without looking as if he were sprawling. He was looking at the wall across the entrance lobby, but he wasn't seeing it. He was half asleep, even though his eyes were wide open, and if the night porter struck a match behind his door, Quillan would know it and bang on his bell.

The brass-trimmed swing doors at the street entrance pushed open and Steve Grayce came in, a summer-weight coat turned up around his neck, his hat yanked low and a cigarette wisping smoke at the corner of his mouth. He looked very casual, very alert, and very much at ease. He strolled over to the desk and rapped on it.

"Wake up!" he snorted.

Quillan moved his eyes an inch and said: "All outside rooms with bath. But positively no parties on the eighth floor. Hiyah, Steve. So you finally got the axe. And for the wrong thing. That's life."

Steve said: "O.K. Have you got a new night man here?"

"Don't need one, Steve. Never did, in my opinion."

"You'll need one as long as old hotel men like you register floozies on the same corridor with people like Leopardi."

Quillan half closed his eyes and then opened them to where they had been before. He said indifferently: "Not me, pal. But anybody can make a mistake. Millar's really an accountant—not a desk man."

Steve leaned back and his face became very still. The smoke almost hung at the tip of his cigarette. His eyes were like black glass now. He smiled a little dishonestly.

"And why was Leopardi put in an eight-dollar room on Eight instead of in a tower suite at twenty-eight per?"

Quillan smiled back at him. "I didn't register Leopardi, old sock. There were reservations in. I supposed they were what he wanted. Some guys don't spend. Any other questions, Mr. Grayce?"

"Yeah. Was Eight-fourteen empty last night?"

"It was on change, so it was empty. Something about the plumbing. Proceed."

"Who marked it on change?"

Quillan's bright fathomless eyes turned and became curiously fixed. He didn't answer.

Steve said: "Here's why. Leopardi was in Eight-fifteen and the two girls in Eight-eleven. Just Eight-thirteen between. A lad with a passkey could have gone into Eight-thirteen and turned both the bolt locks on the communicating doors. Then, if the folks in the two other rooms had done the same thing on their side, they'd have a suite set up."

"So what?" Quillan asked. "We got chiseled out of eight bucks, eh? Well, it happens, in better hotels than this." His eyes looked sleepy now.

Steve said: "Millar could have done that. But hell, it doesn't make sense. Millar's not that kind of a guy. Risk a job for a buck tip—phooey. Millar's no dollar pimp."

Quillan said: "All right, policeman. Tell me what's really on your mind."

"One of the girls in Eight-eleven had a gun. Leopardi got a threat letter yesterday—I don't know where or how. It didn't faze him, though. He tore it up. That's how I know. I collected the pieces from his basket. I suppose Leopardi's boys all checked out of here."

"Of course. They went to the Normandy."

"Call the Normandy, and ask to speak to Leopardi. If he's there, he'll still be at the bottle. Probably with a gang."

"Why?" Quillan asked gently.

"Because you're a nice guy. If Leopardi answers—just hang up." Steve paused and pinched his chin hard. "If he went out, try to find out where."

Quillan straightened, gave Steve another long quiet look and went behind the pebbled-glass screen. Steve stood very still, listening, one hand clenched at his side, the other tapping noiselessly on the marble desk.

In about three minutes Quillan came back and leaned on the desk again and said: "Not there. Party going on in his suite—they sold him a big one—and sounds loud. I talked to a guy who was fairly sober.

He said Leopardi got a call around ten—some girl. He went out preening himself, as the fellow says. Hinting about a very juicy date. The guy was just lit enough to hand me all this."

Steve said: "You're a real pal. I hate not to tell you the rest. Well, I liked working here. Not much work at that."

He started towards the entrance doors again. Quillan let him get his hand on the brass handle before he called out. Steve turned and came back slowly.

Quillan said: "I heard Leopardi took a shot at you. I don't think it was noticed. It wasn't reported down here. And I don't think Peters fully realized that until he saw the mirror in Eight-fifteen. If you care to come back, Steve—"

Steve shook his head. "Thanks for the thought."

"And hearing about that shot," Quillan added, "made me remember something. Two years ago a girl shot herself in Eight-fifteen."

Steve straightened his back so sharply that he almost jumped. "What girl?"

Quillan looked surprised. "I don't know. I don't remember her real name. Some girl who had been kicked around all she could stand and wanted to die in a clean bed—alone."

Steve reached across and took hold of Quillan's arm. "The hotel files," he rasped. "The clippings, whatever there was in the papers will be in them. I want to see those clippings."

Quillan stared at him for a long moment. Then he said: "Whatever game you're playing, kid—you're playing it damn close to your vest. I will say that for you. And me bored stiff with a night to kill."

He reached along the desk and thumped the call bell. The door of the night porter's room opened and the porter came across the entrance lobby. He nodded and smiled at Steve.

Quillan said: "Take the board, Carl. I'll be in Mr. Peters' office for a little while."

He went to the safe and got keys out of it.

# 8

The cabin was high up on the side of the mountain, against a thick growth of digger pine, oak and incense cedar. It was solidly built, with a stone chimney, shingled all over and heavily braced against the slope of the hill. By daylight the roof was green and the sides dark reddish brown and the window frames and draw curtains red. In the uncanny brightness of an all-night mid-October moon in the mountains, it stood out sharply in every detail, except color.

It was at the end of a road, a quarter of a mile from any other cabin. Steve rounded the bend towards it without lights, at five in the morning. He stopped his car at once, when he was sure it was the right cabin, got out and walked soundlessly along the side of the gravel road, on a carpet of wild iris.

On the road level there was a rough pine board garage, and from this a path went up to the cabin porch. The garage was unlocked. Steve swung the door open carefully, groped in past the dark bulk of a car and felt the top of the radiator. It was still warmish. He got a small flash out of his pocket and played it over the car. A gray sedan, dusty, the gas gauge low. He snapped the flash off, shut the garage door carefully and slipped into place the piece of wood that served for a hasp. Then he climbed the path to the house.

There was light behind the drawn red curtains. The porch was high and juniper logs were piled on it, with

the bark still on them. The front door had a thumb
latch and a rustic door handle above.

He went up, neither too softly nor too noisily, lifted
his hand, sighed deep in his throat, and knocked. His
hand touched the butt of the gun in the inside pocket
of his coat, once, then came away empty.

A chair creaked and steps padded across the floor
and a voice called out softly: "What is it?" Millar's
voice.

Steve put his lips close to the wood and said: "This
is Steve, George. You up already?"

The key turned, and the door opened. George Millar, the dapper night auditor of the Carlton House,
didn't look dapper now. He was dressed in old trousers
and a thick blue sweater with a roll collar. His feet
were in ribbed wool socks and fleece-lined slippers. His
clipped black mustache was a curved smudge across his
pale face. Two electric bulbs burned in their sockets in
a low beam across the room, below the slope of the high
roof. A table lamp was lit and its shade was tilted to
throw light on a big Morris chair with a leather seat
and back-cushion. A fire burned lazily in a heap of soft
ash on the big open hearth.

Millar said in his low, husky voice: "Hell's sake,
Steve. Glad to see you. How'd you find us anyway?
Come on in, guy."

Steve stepped through the door and Millar locked it.
"City habit," he said grinning. "Nobody locks anything
in the mountains. Have a chair. Warm your toes.
Cold out at this time of night."

Steve said: "Yeah. Plenty cold."

He sat down in the Morris chair and put his hat and
coat on the end of the solid wood table behind it. He
leaned forward and held his hands out to the fire.

Millar said: "How the hell did you find us, Steve?"

Steve didn't look at him. He said quietly: "Not so

easy at that. You told me last night your brother had a cabin up here—remember? So I had nothing to do, so I thought I'd drive up and bum some breakfast. The guy in the inn at Crestline didn't know who had cabins where. His trade is with people passing through. I rang up a garage man and he didn't know any Millar cabin. Then I saw a light come on down the street in a coal-and-wood yard and a little guy who is forest ranger and deputy sheriff and wood-and-gas dealer and half a dozen other things was getting his car out to go down to San Bernardino for some tank gas. A very smart little guy. The minute I said your brother had been a fighter he wised up. So here I am."

Millar pawed at his mustache. Bedsprings creaked at the back of the cabin somewhere. "Sure, he still goes under his fighting name—Gaff Talley. I'll get him up and we'll have some coffee. I guess you and me are both in the same boat. Used to working at night and can't sleep. I haven't been to bed at all."

Steve looked at him slowly and looked away. A burly voice behind them said: "Gaff is up. Who's your pal, George?"

Steve stood up casually and turned. He looked at the man's hands first. He couldn't help himself. They were large hands, well kept as to cleanliness, but coarse and ugly. One knuckle had been broken badly. He was a big man with reddish hair. He wore a sloppy bathrobe over outing-flannel pajamas. He had a leathery expressionless face, scarred over the cheekbones. There were fine white scars over his eyebrows and at the corners of his mouth. His nose was spread and thick. His whole face looked as if it had caught a lot of gloves. His eyes alone looked vaguely like Millar's eyes.

Millar said: "Steve Grayce. Night man at the hotel—until last night." His grin was a little vague.

Gaff Talley came over and shook hands. "Glad to

meet you," he said. "I'll get some duds on and we'll scrape a breakfast off the shelves. I slept enough. George ain't slept any, the poor sap."

He went back across the room towards the door through which he'd come. He stopped there and leaned on an old phonograph, put his big hand down behind a pile of records in paper envelopes. He stayed just like that, without moving.

Millar said: "Any luck on a job, Steve? Or did you try yet?"

"Yeah. In a way. I guess I'm a sap, but I'm going to have a shot at the private-agency racket. Not much in it unless I can land some publicity." He shrugged. Then he said very quietly: "King Leopardi's been bumped off."

Millar's mouth snapped wide open. He stayed like that for almost a minute—perfectly still, with his mouth open. Gaff Talley leaned against the wall and stared without showing anything in his face. Millar finally said: "Bumped off? Where? Don't tell me—"

"Not in the hotel, George. Too bad, wasn't it? In a girl's apartment. Nice girl too. She didn't entice him there. The old suicide gag—only it won't work. And the girl is my client."

Millar didn't move. Neither did the big man. Steve leaned his shoulders against the stone mantel. He said softly: "I went out to the Club Shalotte this afternoon to apologize to Leopardi. Silly idea, because I didn't owe him an apology. There was a girl there in the bar lounge with him. He took three socks at me and left. The girl didn't like that. We got rather clubby. Had a drink together. Then late tonight—last night—she called me up and said Leopardi was over at her place and he was drunk and she couldn't get rid of him. I went there. Only he wasn't drunk. He was dead, in her bed, in yellow pajamas."

The big man lifted his left hand and roughed back his hair. Millar leaned slowly against the edge of the table, as if he were afraid the edge might be sharp enough to cut him. His mouth twitched under the clipped black mustache."

He said huskily: "That's lousy."

The big man said: "Well, for cryin' into a milk bottle."

Steve said: "Only they weren't Leopardi's pajamas. His had initials on them—big black initials. And his were satin, not silk. And although he had a gun in his hand—this girl's gun by the way—*he* didn't shoot himself in the heart. The cops will determine that. Maybe you birds never heard of the Lund test, with paraffin wax, to find out who did or didn't fire a gun recently. The kill ought to have been pulled in the hotel last night, in Room Eight-fifteen. I spoiled that by heaving him out on his neck before that black-haired girl in Eight-eleven could get to him. Didn't I, George?"

Millar said: "I guess you did—if I know what you're talking about."

Steve said slowly: "I think you know what I'm talking about, George. It would have been a kind of poetic justice if King Leopardi had been knocked off in Room Eight-fifteen. Because that was the room where a girl shot herself two years ago. A girl who registered as Mary Smith—but whose usual name was Eve Talley. And whose real name was Eve Millar."

The big man leaned heavily on the victrola and said thickly: "Maybe I ain't woke up yet. That sounds like it might grow up to be a dirty crack. We had a sister named Eve that shot herself in the Carlton. So what?"

Steve smiled a little crookedly. He said: "Listen, George. You told me Quillan registered those girls in Eight-eleven. *You* did. You told me Leopardi registered on Eight, instead of in a good suite, because he was tight. He wasn't tight. He just didn't care where he was put, as long as female company was handy. And you saw to that. You planned the whole thing, George. You even got Peters to write Leopardi at the Raleigh in Frisco and ask him to use the Carlton when he came down—because the same man owned it who owned the Club Shalotte. As if a guy like Jumbo Walters would care where a bandleader registered."

Millar's face was dead white, expressionless. His voice cracked. "Steve—for God's sake, Steve, what are you talking about? How the hell could I—"

"Sorry, kid. I liked working with you. I liked you a lot. I guess I still like you. But I don't like people who strangle women—or people who smear women in order to cover up a revenge murder."

His hand shot up—and stopped. The big man said: "Take it easy—and look at this one."

Gaff's hand had come up from behind the pile of records. A Colt .45 was in it. He said between his teeth: "I always thought house dicks were just a bunch of cheap grafters. I guess I missed out on you. You got a few brains. Hell, I bet you even run out to One-eighteen Court Street. Right?"

Steve let his hand fall empty and looked straight at the big Colt. "Right. I saw the girl—dead—with your fingers marked into her neck. They can measure those, fella. Killing Dolores Chiozza's maid the same way was a mistake. They'll match up the two sets of marks, find out that your black-haired gun girl was at the Carlton last night, and piece the whole story together. With the information they get at the hotel they can't miss. I give you two weeks, if you beat it quick. And I mean quick."

Millar licked his dry lips and said softly: "There's no hurry, Steve. No hurry at all. Our job is done.

Maybe not the best way, maybe not the nicest way, but it wasn't a nice job. And Leopardi was the worst kind of a louse. We loved our sister, and he made a tramp out of her. She was a wide-eyed kid that fell for a flashy greaseball, and the greaseball went up in the world and threw her out on her ear for a red-headed torcher who was more his kind. He threw her out and broke her heart and she killed herself."

Steve said harshly: "Yeah—and what were you doing all that time—manicuring your nails?"

"We weren't around when it happened. It took us a little time to find out the why of it."

Steve said: "So that was worth killing four people for, was it? And as for Dolores Chiozza, she wouldn't have wiped her feet on Leopardi—then, or any time since. But you had to put her in the middle too, with your rotten little revenge murder. You make me sick, George. Tell your big tough brother to get on with his murder party."

The big man grinned and said: "Nuff talk, George. See has he a gat—and don't get behind him or in front of him. This bean-shooter goes on through."

Steve stared at the big man's .45. His face was hard as white bone. There was a thin cold sneer on his lips and his eyes were cold and dark.

Millar moved softly in his fleece-lined slippers. He came around the end of the table and went close to Steve's side and reached out a hand to tap his pockets. He stepped back and pointed: "In there."

Steve said softly: "I must be nuts. I could have taken you then, George."

Gaff Talley barked: "Stand away from him."

He walked solidly across the room and put the big Colt against Steve's stomach hard. He reached up with his left hand and worked the Detective Special from the inside breast pocket. His eyes were sharp on

Steve's eyes. He held Steve's gun out behind him. "Take this, George."

Millar took the gun and went over beyond the big table again and stood at the far corner of it. Gaff Talley backed away from Steve.

"You're through, wise guy," he said. "You got to know that. There's only two ways outa these mountains and we gotta have time. And maybe you didn't tell nobody. See?"

Steve stood like a rock, his face white, a twisted half-smile working at the corners of his lips. He stared hard at the big man's gun and his stare was faintly puzzled.

Millar said: "Does it have to be that way, Gaff?" His voice was a croak now, without tone, without its usual pleasant huskiness.

Steve turned his head a little and looked at Millar. "Sure it has, George. You're just a couple of cheap hoodlums after all. A couple of nasty-minded sadists playing at being revengers of wronged girlhood. Hill-billy stuff. And right this minute you're practically cold meat—cold, rotten meat."

Gaff Talley laughed and cocked the big revolver with his thumb. "Say your prayers, guy," he jeered.

Steve said grimly: "What makes you think you're going to bump me off with that thing? No shells in it, strangler. Better try to take me the way you handle women—with your hands."

The big man's eyes flicked down, clouded. Then he roared with laughter. "Geez, the dust on that one must be a foot thick," he chuckled. "Watch."

He pointed the big gun at the floor and squeezed the trigger. The firing pin clicked dryly—on an empty chamber. The big man's face convulsed.

For a short moment nobody moved. Then Gaff

turned slowly on the balls of his feet and looked at his brother. He said almost gently: "You, George?"

Millar licked his lips and gulped. He had to move his mouth in and out before he could speak.

"Me. Gaff. I was standing by the window when Steve got out of his car down the road, I saw him go into the garage. I knew the car would still be warm. There's been enough killing, Gaff. Too much. So I took the shells out of your gun."

Millar's thumb moved back the hammer on the Detective Special. Gaff's eyes bulged. He stared fascinated at the snub-nosed gun. Then he lunged violently towards it, flailing with the empty Colt. Millar braced himself and stood very still and said dimly, like an old man: "Goodbye, Gaff."

The gun jumped three times in his small neat hand. Smoke curled lazily from its muzzle. A piece of burned log fell over in the fireplace.

Gaff Talley smiled queerly and stooped and stood perfectly still. The gun dropped at his feet. He put his big heavy hands against his stomach, said slowly, thickly: "'S all right, kid. 'S all right, I guess . . . I guess I . . ."

His voice trailed off and his legs began to twist under him. Steve took three long quick silent steps, and slammed Millar hard on the angle of the jaw. The big man was still falling—as slowly as a tree falls.

Millar spun across the room and crashed against the end wall and a blue-and-white plate fell off the plate-molding and broke. The gun sailed from his fingers. Steve dived for it and came up with it. Millar crouched and watched his brother.

Gaff Talley bent his head to the floor and braced his hands and then lay down quietly, on his stomach, like a man who was very tired. He made no sound of any kind.

Daylight showed at the windows, around the red glass-curtains. The piece of broken log smoked against the side of the hearth and the rest of the fire was a heap of soft gray ash with a glow at its heart.

Steve said dully: "You saved my life, George—or at least you saved a lot of shooting. I took the chance because what I wanted was evidence. Step over there to the desk and write it all out and sign it."

Millar said: "Is he dead?"

"He's dead, George. You killed him. Write that too."

Millar said quietly: "It's funny. I wanted to finish Leopardi myself, with my own hands, when he was at the top, when he had the farthest to fall. Just finish him and then take what came. But Gaff was the guy who wanted it done cute. Gaff, the tough mug who never had any education and never dodged a punch in his life, wanted to do it smart and figure angles. Well, maybe that's why he owned property, like that apartment house on Court Street that Jake Stoyanoff managed for him. I don't know how he got to Dolores Chiozza's maid. It doesn't matter much, does it?"

Steve said: "Go and write it. You were the one called Leopardi up and pretended to be the girl, huh?"

Millar said: "Yes. I'll write it all down, Steve. I'll sign it and then you'll let me go—just for an hour. Won't you, Steve? Just an hour's start. That's not much to ask of an old friend, is it, Steve?"

Millar smiled. It was a small, frail, ghostly smile. Steve bent beside the big sprawled man and felt his neck artery. He looked up, said: "Quite dead . . . Yes, you get an hour's start, George—if you write it all out."

Millar walked softly over to a tall oak highboy desk, studded with tarnished brass nails. He opened the flap and sat down and reached for a pen. He unscrewed the top from a bottle of ink and began to write in his neat, clear accountant's handwriting.

Steve Grayce sat down in front of the fire and lit a cigarette and stared at the ashes. He held the gun with his left hand on his knee. Outside the cabin, birds began to sing. Inside there was no sound but the scratching pen.

## 9

The sun was well up when Steve left the cabin, locked it up, walked down the steep path and along the narrow gravel road to his car. The garage was empty now. The gray sedan was gone. Smoke from another cabin floated lazily above the pines and oaks half a mile away. He started his car, drove it around a bend, past two old boxcars that had been converted into cabins, then on to a main road with a stripe down the middle and so up the hill to Crestline.

He parked on the main street before the Rim-of-the-World Inn, had a cup of coffee at the counter, then shut himself in a phone booth at the back of the empty lounge. He had the long distance operator get Jumbo Walters' number in Los Angeles, then called the owner of the Club Shalotte.

A voice said silkily: "This is Mr. Walters' residence."

"Steve Grayce. Put him on, if you please."

"One moment, please." A click, another voice, not so smooth and much harder. "Yeah?"

"Steve Grayce. I want to speak to Mr. Walters."

"Sorry. I don't seem to know you. It's a little early, amigo. What's your business?"

"Did he go to Miss Chiozza's place?"

"Oh." A pause. "The shamus. I get it. Hold the line, pal."

Another voice now—lazy, with the faintest color of Irish in it. "You can talk, son. This is Walters."

"I'm Steve Grayce. I'm the man—"

"I know all about that, son. The lady is O.K., by the way. I think she's asleep upstairs. Go on."

"I'm at Crestline—top of the Arrowhead grade. Two men murdered Leopardi. One was George Millar, night auditor at the Carlton Hotel. The other his brother, an ex-fighter named Gaff Talley. Talley's dead—shot by his brother. Millar got away—but he left me a full confession signed, detailed, complete."

Walters said slowly: "You're a fast worker, son— unless you're just plain crazy. Better come in here fast. Why did they do it?"

"They had a sister."

Walters repeated quietly: "They had a sister . . . What about this fellow that got away? We don't want some hick sheriff or publicity-hungry county attorney to get ideas—"

Steve broke in quietly: "I don't think you'll have to worry about that, Mr. Walters. I think I know where he's gone."

He ate breakfast at the inn, not because he was hungry, but because he was weak. He got into his car again and started down the long smooth grade from Crestline to San Bernardino, a broad paved boulevard skirting the edge of a sheer drop into the deep valley. There were places where the road went close to the edge, white guard-fences alongside.

Two miles below Crestline was the place. The road made a sharp turn around a shoulder of the mountain. Cars were parked on the gravel off the pavement—several private cars, an official car, and a wrecking car. The white fence was broken through and men stood around the broken place looking down.

Eight hundred feet below, what was left of a gray sedan lay silent and crumpled in the morning sunshine.

# PEARLS ARE A NUISANCE

IT IS QUITE TRUE that I wasn't doing anything that morning except looking at a blank sheet of paper in my typewriter and thinking about writing a letter. It is also quite true that I don't have a great deal to do any morning. But that is no reason why I should have to go out hunting for old Mrs. Penruddock's pearl necklace. I don't happen to be a policeman.

It was Ellen Macintosh who called me up, which made a difference, of course. "How are you, darling?" she asked. "Busy?"

"Yes and no," I said. "Mostly no. I am very well. What is it now?"

"I don't think you love me, Walter. And anyway you ought to get some work to do. You have too much money. Somebody has stolen Mrs. Penruddock's pearls and I want you to find them."

"Possibly you think you have the police department on the line," I said coldly. "This is the residence of Walter Gage. Mr. Gage talking."

"Well, you can tell Mr. Gage from Miss Ellen Macin-

163

tosh," she said, "that if he is not out here in half an hour, he will receive a small parcel by registered mail containing one diamond engagement ring."

"And a lot of good it did me," I said. "That old crow will live for another fifty years."

But she had already hung up so I put my hat on and went down and drove off in the Packard. It was a nice late April morning, if you care for that sort of thing. Mrs. Penruddock lived on a wide quiet street in Carondelet Park. The house had probably looked exactly the same for the last fifty years, but that didn't make me any better pleased that Ellen Macintosh might live in it another fifty years, unless old Mrs. Penruddock died and didn't need a nurse any more. Mr. Penruddock had died a few years before, leaving no will, a thoroughly tangled-up estate, and a list of pensioners as long as a star boarder's arm.

I rang the front doorbell and the door was opened, not very soon, by a little old woman with a maid's apron and a strangled knot of gray hair on the top of her head. She looked at me as if she had never seen me before and didn't want to see me now.

"Miss Ellen Macintosh, please," I said. "Mr. Walter Gage calling."

She sniffed, turned without a word and we went back into the musty recesses of the house and came to a glassed-in porch full of wicker furniture and the smell of Egyptian tombs. She went away, with another sniff.

In a moment the door opened again and Ellen Macintosh came in. Maybe you don't like tall girls with honey-colored hair and skin like the first strawberry peach the grocer sneaks out of the box for himself. If you don't, I'm sorry for you.

"Darling, so you did come," she cried. "That was nice of you, Walter. Now sit down and I'll tell you all about it."

We sat down.

"Mrs. Penruddock's pearl necklace has been stolen, Walter."

"You told me that over the telephone. My temperature is still normal."

"If you will excuse a professional guess," she said, "it is probably subnormal—permanently. The pearls are a string of forty-nine matched pink ones which Mr. Penruddock gave to Mrs. Penruddock for her golden wedding present. She hardly ever wore them lately, except perhaps on Christmas or when she had a couple of very old friends in to dinner and was well enough to sit up. And every Thanksgiving she gives a dinner to all the pensioners and friends and old employees Mr. Penruddock left on her hands, and she wore them then."

"You are getting your verb tenses a little mixed," I said, "but the general idea is clear. Go on."

"Well, Walter," Ellen said, with what some people call an arch look, "the pearls have been stolen. Yes, I know that is the third time I told you that, but there's a strange mystery about it. They were kept in a leather case in an old safe which was open half the time and which I should judge a strong man could open with his fingers even when it was locked. I had to go there for a paper this morning and I looked in at the pearls just to say hello—"

"I hope your idea in hanging on to Mrs. Penruddock has not been that she might leave you that necklace," I said stiffly. "Pearls are all very well for old people and fat blondes, but for tall willowy—"

"Oh shut up, darling," Ellen broke in. "I should certainly not have been waiting for these pearls—because they were false."

I swallowed hard and stared at her. "Well," I said, with a leer, "I have heard that old Penruddock pulled some cross-eyed rabbits out of the hat occasionally, but giving his own wife a string of phony pearls on her golden wedding gets my money."

"Oh, don't be such a fool, Walter! They were real enough then. The fact is Mrs. Penruddock sold them and had imitations made. One of her old friends, Mr. Lansing Gallemore of the Gallemore Jewelry Company, handled it all for her very quietly, because of course she didn't want anyone to know. And that is why the police have not been called in. You *will* find them for her, won't you, Walter?"

"How? And what did she sell them for?"

"Because Mr. Penruddock died suddenly without making any provision for all these people he had been supporting. Then the depression came, and there was hardly any money at all. Only just enough to carry on the household and pay the servants, all of whom have been with Mrs. Penruddock so long that she would rather starve than let any of them go."

"That's different," I said. "I take my hat off to her. But how the dickens am I going to find them, and what does it matter anyway—if they were false?"

"Well, the pearls—imitations, I mean—cost two hundred dollars and were specially made in Bohemia and it took several months and the way things are over there now she might never be able to get another set of really good imitations. And she is terrified somebody will find out they were false, or that the thief will blackmail her, when he finds out they were false. You see, darling, I know who stole them."

I said, "Huh?" a word I very seldom use as I do not think it part of the vocabulary of a gentleman.

"The chauffeur we had here a few months, Walter— a horrid big brute named Henry Eichelberger. He left suddenly the day before yesterday, for no reason at all. Nobody ever leaves Mrs. Penruddock. Her last chauffeur was a very old man and he died. But Henry Eichelberger left without a word and I'm sure he had stolen the pearls. He tried to kiss me once, Walter."

"Oh, he did," I said in a different voice. "Tried to kiss you, eh? Where is this big slab of meat, darling? Have you any idea at all? It seems hardly likely he would be hanging around on the street corner for me to punch his nose for him."

Ellen lowered her long silky eyelashes at me—and when she does that I go limp as a scrubwoman's back hair.

"He didn't run away. He must have known the pearls were false and that he was safe enough to blackmail Mrs. Penruddock. I called up the agency he came from and he has been back there and registered again for employment. But they said it was against their rules to give his address."

"Why couldn't somebody else have taken the pearls? A burglar, for instance?"

"There is no one else. The servants are beyond suspicion and the house is locked up as tight as an icebox every night and there were no signs of anybody having broken in. Besides Henry Eichelberger knew where the pearls were kept, because he saw me putting them away after the last time she wore them—which was when she had two very dear friends in to dinner on the occasion of the anniversary of Mr. Penruddock's death."

"That must have been a pretty wild party," I said. "All right, I'll go down to the agency and make them give me his address. Where is it?"

"It is called the Ada Twomey Domestic Employment Agency, and it is in the two-hundred block on East Second, a very unpleasant neighborhood."

"Not half as unpleasant as my neighborhood will be

to Henry Eichelberger," I said. "So he tried to kiss you, eh?"

"The pearls, Walter," Ellen said gently, "are the important thing. I do hope he hasn't already found out they are false and thrown them in the ocean."

"If he has, I'll make him dive for them."

"He is six feet three and very big and strong, Walter," Ellen said coyly. "But not handsome like you, of course."

"Just my size," I said. "It will be a pleasure. Goodbye, darling."

She took hold of my sleeve. "There is just one thing, Walter. I don't mind a little fighting because it is manly. But you mustn't cause a disturbance that would bring the police in, you know. And although you are very big and strong and played right tackle at college, you are a little weak about one thing. Will you promise me not to drink any whiskey?"

"This Eichelberger," I said, "is all the drink I want."

## 2

The Ada Twomey Domestic Employment Agency on East Second Street proved to be all that the name and location implied. The odor of the anteroom, in which I was compelled to wait for a short time, was not at all pleasant. The agency was presided over by a hard-faced middle-aged woman who said that Henry Eichelberger was registered with them for employment as a chauffeur, and that she could arrange to have him call upon me, or could bring him there to the office for an interview. But when I placed a ten-dollar bill on her desk and indicated that it was merely an earnest of good faith, without prejudice to any commission which might become due to her agency, she relented and gave me his address, which was out west on Santa

Monica Boulevard, near the part of the city which used to be called Sherman.

I drove out there without delay, for fear that Henry Eichelberger might telephone in and be informed that I was coming. The address proved to be a seedy hotel, conveniently close to the interurban car tracks and having its entrance adjoining a Chinese laundry. The hotel was upstairs, the steps being covered—in places—with strips of decayed rubber matting to which were screwed irregular fragments of unpolished brass. The smell of the Chinese laundry ceased about halfway up the stairs and was replaced by a smell of kerosene, cigar butts, slept-in air and greasy paper bags. There was a register at the head of the stairs on a wooden shelf. The last entry was in pencil, three weeks previous as to date, and had been written by someone with a very unsteady hand. I deduced from this that the management was not over-particular.

There was a bell beside the book and a sign reading: MANAGER. I rang the bell and waited. Presently a door opened down the hall and feet shuffled towards me without haste. A man appeared wearing frayed leather slippers and trousers of a nameless color, which had the two top buttons unlatched to permit more freedom to the suburbs of his extensive stomach. He also wore red suspenders, his shirt was darkened under the arms, and elsewhere, and his face badly needed a thorough laundering and trimming.

He said, "Full-up, bud," and sneered.

I said: "I am not looking for a room. I am looking for one Eichelberger, who, I am informed lives here, but who, I observe, has not registered in your book. And this, as of course you know, is contrary to the law."

"A wise guy," the fat man sneered again. "Down the

hall, bud. Two-eighteen." He waved a thumb the color and almost the size of a burnt baked potato.

"Have the kindness to show me the way," I said.

"Geez, the lootenant-governor," he said, and began to shake his stomach. His small eyes disappeared in folds of yellow fat. "O.K., bud. Follow on."

We went into the gloomy depths of the back hall and came to a wooden door at the end with a closed wooden transom above it. The fat man smote the door with a fat hand. Nothing happened.

"Out," he said.

"Have the kindness to unlock the door," I said. "I wish to go in and wait for Eichelberger."

"In a pig's valise," the fat man said nastily. "Who the hell you think you are, bum?"

This angered me. He was a fair-sized man, about six feet tall, but too full of the memories of beer. I looked up and down the dark hall. The place seemed utterly deserted.

I hit the fat man in the stomach.

He sat down on the floor and belched and his right kneecap came into sharp contact with his jaw. He coughed and tears welled up in his eyes.

"Cripes, bud," he whined. "You got twenty years on me. That ain't fair."

"Open the door," I said. "I have no time to argue with you."

"A buck," he said, wiping his eyes on his shirt. "Two bucks and no tip-off."

I took two dollars out of my pocket and helped the man to his feet. He folded the two dollars and produced an ordinary passkey which I could have purchased for five cents.

"Brother, you sock," he said. "Where you learn it? Most big guys are muscle-bound." He unlocked the door.

"If you hear any noises later on," I said, "ignore them. If there is any damage, it will be paid for generously."

He nodded and I went into the room. He locked the door behind me and his steps receded. There was silence.

The room was small, mean and tawdry. It contained a brown chest of drawers with a small mirror hanging over it, a straight wooden chair, a wooden rocking chair, a single bed of chipped enamel, with a much mended cotton counterpane. The curtains at the single window had fly marks on them and the green shade was without a slat at the bottom. There was a wash bowl in the corner with two paper-thin towels hanging beside it. There was, of course, no bathroom, and there was no closet. A piece of dark figured material hanging from a shelf made a substitute for the latter. Behind this I found a gray business suit of the largest size made, which would be my size, if I wore ready-made clothes, which I do not. There was a pair of black brogues on the floor, size number twelve at least. There was also a cheap fiber suitcase, which of course I searched, as it was not locked.

I also searched the bureau and was surprised to find that everything in it was neat and clean and decent. But there was not much in it. Particularly there were no pearls in it. I searched in all other likely and unlikely places in the room but I found nothing of interest.

I sat on the side of the bed and lit a cigarette and waited. It was now apparent to me that Henry Eichelberger was either a very great fool or entirely innocent. The room and the open trail he had left behind him did not suggest a man dealing in operations like stealing pearl necklaces.

I had smoked four cigarettes, more than I usually smoke in an entire day, when approaching steps sounded. They were light quick steps but not at all clandestine. A key was thrust into the door and turned and the door swung carelessly open. A man stepped through it and looked at me.

I am six feet three inches in height and weigh over two hundred pounds. This man was tall, but he seemed lighter. He wore a blue serge suit of the kind which is called neat for lack of anything better to say about it. He had thick wiry blond hair, a neck like a Prussian corporal in a cartoon, very wide shoulders and large hard hands, and he had a face that had taken much battering in its time. His small greenish eyes glinted at me with what I then took to be evil humor. I saw at once that he was not a man to trifle with, but I was not afraid of him. I was his equal in size and strength, and, I had small doubt, his superior in intelligence.

I stood up off the bed calmly and said: "I am looking for one Eichelberger."

"How you get in here, bud?" It was a cheerful voice, rather heavy, but not unpleasant to the ear.

"The explanation of that can wait," I said stiffly. "I am looking for one Eichelberger. Are you he?"

"Haw," the man said. "A gut-buster. A comedian. Wait'll I loosen my belt." He took a couple of steps farther into the room and I took the same number towards him.

"My name is Walter Gage," I said. "Are you Eichelberger?"

"Gimme a nickel," he said, "and I'll tell you."

I ignored that. "I am the fiancé of Miss Ellen Macintosh," I told him coldly. "I am informed that you tried to kiss her."

He took another step towards me and I another towards him. "Whaddaya mean—tried?" he sneered.

I led sharply with my right and it landed flush on his chin. It seemed to me a good solid punch, but it scarcely moved him. I then put two hard left jabs into his neck and landed a second hard right at the side of his rather wide nose. He snorted and hit me in the solar plexus.

I bent over and took hold of the room with both hands and spun it. When I had it nicely spinning I gave it a full swing and hit myself on the back of the head with the floor. This made me lose my balance temporarily and while I was thinking about how to regain it a wet towel began to slap at my face and I opened my eyes. The face of Henry Eichelberger was close to mine and bore a certain appearance of solicitude.

"Bud," his voice said, "your stomach is as weak as a Chinaman's tea."

"Brandy!" I croaked. "What happened?"

"You tripped on a little tear in the carpet, bud. You really got to have liquor?"

"Brandy," I croaked again, and closed my eyes.

"I hope it don't get me started," his voice said.

A door opened and closed. I lay motionless and tried to avoid being sick at my stomach. The time passed slowly, in a long gray veil. Then the door of the room opened and closed once more and a moment later something hard was being pressed against my lips. I opened my mouth and liquor poured down my throat. I coughed, but the fiery liquid coursed through my veins and strengthened me at once. I sat up.

"Thank you, Henry," I said. "May I call you Henry?"

"No tax on it, bud."

I got to my feet and stood before him. He stared at me curiously. "You look O.K.," he said. "Why'n't you told me you was sick?"

"Damn you, Eichelberger!" I said and hit with all my strength on the side of his jaw. He shook his head and his eyes seemed annoyed. I delivered three more punches to his face and jaw while he was still shaking his head.

"So you wanta play for keeps!" he yelled and took hold of the bed and threw it at me.

I dodged the corner of the bed, but in doing so I moved a little too quickly and lost my balance and pushed my head about four inches into the baseboard under the window.

A wet towel began to slap at my face. I opened my eyes.

"Listen, kid. You got two strikes and no balls on you. Maybe you oughta try a lighter bat."

"Brandy," I croaked.

"You'll take rye." He pressed a glass against my lips and I drank thirstily. Then I climbed to my feet again.

The bed, to my astonishment, had not moved. I sat down on it and Henry Eichelberger sat down beside me and patted my shoulder.

"You and me could get along," he said. "I never kissed your girl, although I ain't saying I wouldn't like to. Is that all is worrying at you?"

He poured himself half a waterglassful of the whiskey out of the pint bottle which he had gone out to buy. He swallowed the liquor thoughtfully.

"No, there is another matter," I said.

"Shoot. But no more haymakers. Promise?"

I promised him rather reluctantly. "Why did you leave the employ of Mrs. Penruddock?" I asked him.

He looked at me from under his shaggy blond eyebrows. Then he looked at the bottle he was holding in his hand. "Would you call me a looker?" he asked.

"Well, Henry—"

"Don't pansy up on me," he snarled.

"No, Henry, I should not call you very handsome. But unquestionably you are virile."

He poured another half-waterglassful of whiskey and handed it to me. "Your turn," he said. I drank it down without fully realizing what I was doing. When I had stopped coughing Henry took the glass out of my hand and refilled it. He took his own drink moodily. The bottle was now nearly empty.

"Suppose you fell for a dame with all the looks this side of heaven. With a map like mine. A guy like me, a guy from the stockyards that played himself a lot of very tough left end at a cow college and left his looks and education on the scoreboard. A guy that has fought everything but whales and freight hogs—engines to you —and licked 'em all, but naturally had to take a sock now and then. Then I get a job where I see this lovely all the time and every day and know it's no dice. What would you do, pal? Me, I just quit the job."

"Henry, I'd like to shake your hand," I said.

He shook hands with me listlessly. "So I ask for my time," he said. "What else would I do?" He held the bottle up and looked at it against the light. "Bo, you made an error when you had me get this. When I start drinking it's a world cruise. You got plenty dough?"

"Certainly," I said. "If whiskey is what you want, Henry, whiskey is what you shall have. I have a very nice apartment on Franklin Avenue in Hollywood and while I cast no aspersions on your own humble and of course quite temporary abode, I now suggest we repair to my apartment, which is a good deal larger and gives one more room to extend one's elbow." I waved my hand airily.

"Say, you're drunk," Henry said, with admiration in his small green eyes.

"I am not yet drunk, Henry, although I do in fact feel the effect of that whiskey and very pleasantly. You must not mind my way of talking which is a personal matter, like your own clipped and concise method of speech. But before we depart there is one other rather insignificant detail I wish to discuss with you. I am empowered to arrange for the return of Mrs. Penruddock's pearls. I understand there is some possibility that you may have stolen them."

"Son, you take some awful chances," Henry said softly.

"This is a business matter, Henry, and plain talk is the best way to settle it. The pearls are only false pearls, so we should very easily be able to come to an agreement. I mean you no ill will, Henry, and I am obliged to you for procuring the whiskey, but business is business. Will you take fifty dollars and return the pearls and no questions asked?"

Henry laughed shortly and mirthlessly, but he seemed to have no animosity in his voice when he said: "So you think I stole some marbles and am sitting around here waiting for a flock of dicks to swarm me?"

"No police have been told, Henry, and you may not have known the pearls were false. Pass the liquor, Henry."

He poured me most of what was left in the bottle, and I drank it down with the greatest good humor. I threw the glass at the mirror, but unfortunately missed. The glass, which was of heavy and cheap construction, fell on the floor and did not break. Henry Eichelberger laughed heartily.

"What are you laughing at, Henry?"

"Nothing," he said. "I was just thinking what a sucker some guy is finding out he is—about them marbles."

"You mean you did not steal the pearls, Henry?"

He laughed again, a little gloomily. "Yeah," he said, "meaning no. I oughta sock you, but what the hell? Any guy can get a bum idea. No, I didn't steal no pearls, bud. If they was ringers, I wouldn't be bothered, and if they was what they looked like the one time I saw them on the old lady's neck, I wouldn't decidedly be holed up in no cheap flot in L.A. waiting for a couple carloads of johns to put the sneeze on me."

I reached for his hand again and shook it.

"That is all I required to know," I said happily. "Now I am at peace. We shall now go to my apartment and consider ways and means to recover these pearls. You and I together should make a team that can conquer any opposition, Henry."

"You ain't kidding me, huh?"

I stood up and put my hat on—upside down. "No, Henry. I am making you an offer of employment which I understand you need, and all the whiskey you can drink. Let us go. Can you drive a car in your condition?"

"Hell, I ain't drunk," Henry said, looking surprised.

We left the room and walked down the dark hallway. The fat manager very suddenly appeared from some nebulous shade and stood in front of us rubbing his stomach and looking at me with small greedy expectant eyes. "Everything oke?" he inquired, chewing on a time-darkened toothpick.

"Give him a buck," Henry said.

"What for, Henry?"

"Oh, I dunno. Just give him a buck."

I withdrew a dollar bill from my pocket and gave it to the fat man.

"Thanks, pal," Henry said. He chucked the fat man under the Adam's apple, and removed the dollar bill deftly from between his fingers. "That pays for the hooch," he added. "I hate to have to bum dough."

We went down the stairs arm in arm, leaving the manager trying to cough the toothpick up from his esophagus.

## 3

At five o'clock that afternoon I awoke from slumber and found that I was lying on my bed in my apartment in the Chateau Moraine, on Franklin Avenue near Ivar Street, in Hollywood. I turned my head, which ached, and saw that Henry Eichelberger was lying beside me in his undershirt and trousers. I then perceived that I also was as lightly attired. On the table near by there stood an almost full bottle of Old Pantation rye whiskey, the full quart size, and on the floor lay an entirely empty bottle of the same excellent brand. There were garments lying here and there on the floor, and a cigarette had burned a hole in the brocaded arm of one of my easy chairs.

I felt myself over carefully. My stomach was stiff and sore and my jaw seemed a little swollen on one side. Otherwise I was none the worse for wear. A sharp pain darted through my temples as I stood up off the bed, but I ignored it and walked steadily to the bottle on the table and raised it to my lips. After a steady draught of the fiery liquid I suddenly felt much better. A hearty and cheerful mood came over me and I was ready for any adventure. I went back to the bed and shook Henry firmly by the shoulder.

"Wake up, Henry," I said. "The sunset hour is nigh. The robins are calling and the squirrels are scolding and the morning glories furl themselves in sleep."

Like all men of action Henry Eichelberger came awake with his fist doubled. "What was that crack?" he snarled. "Oh, yeah. Hi, Walter. How you feel?"

"I feel splendid. Are you rested?"

"Sure." He swung his shoeless feet to the floor and rumpled his thick blond hair with his fingers. "We was going swell until you passed out," he said. "So I had me a nap. I never drink solo. You O.K.?"

"Yes, Henry, I feel very well indeed. And we have work to do."

"Swell." He went to the whiskey bottle and quaffed from it freely. He rubbed his stomach with the flat of his hand. His green eyes shone peacefully. "I'm a sick man," he said, "and I got to take my medicine." He put the bottle down on the table and surveyed the apartment. "Geez," he said, "we thrown it into us so fast I ain't hardly looked at the dump. You got a nice little place here, Walter. Geez, a white typewriter and a white telephone. What's the matter, kid—you just been confirmed?"

"Just a foolish fancy, Henry," I said, waving an airy hand.

Henry went over and looked at the typewriter and the telephone side by side on my writing desk, and the silver-mounted desk set, each piece chased with my initials.

"Well fixed, huh?" Henry said, turning his green gaze on me.

"Tolerably so, Henry," I said modestly.

"Well, what next pal? You got any ideas or do we just drink some?"

"Yes, Henry, I do have an idea. With a man like you to help me I think it can be put into practice. I feel that we must, as they say, tap the grapevine. When a string of pearls is stolen, all the underworld knows it at once. Pearls are hard to sell, Henry, inasmuch as they cannot be cut and can be identified by experts, I have read. The underworld will be seething with activity. It should not be too difficult for us to find someone who would send a message to the proper quarter that we are willing to pay a reasonable sum for their return."

"You talk nice—for a drunk guy," Henry said,

reaching for the bottle. "But ain't you forgot these marbles are phonies?"

"For sentimental reasons I am quite willing to pay for their return, just the same."

Henry drank some whiskey, appeared to enjoy the flavor of it and drank some more. He waved the bottle at me politely.

"That's O.K.—as far as it goes," he said. "But this underworld that's doing all this here seething you spoke of ain't going to seethe a hell of a lot over a string of glass beads. Or am I screwy?"

"I was thinking, Henry, that the underworld probably has a sense of humor and the laugh that would go around would be quite emphatic."

"There's an idea in that," Henry said. "Here's some mug finds out lady Penruddock has a string of oyster fruit worth oodles of kale, and he does hisself a neat little box job and trots down to the fence. And the fence gives him the belly laugh. I would say something like that could get around the poolrooms and start a little idle chatter. So far, so nutty. But this box man is going to dump them beads in a hurry, because he has a three-to-ten on him even if they are only worth a nickel plus sales tax. Breaking and entering is the rap, Walter."

"However, Henry," I said, "there is another element in the situation. If this thief is very stupid, it will not, of course, have much weight. But if he is even moderately intelligent, it will. Mrs. Penruddock is a very proud woman and lives in a very exclusive section of the city. If it should become known that she wore imitation pearls, and above all, if it should be even hinted in the public press that these were the very pearls her own husband had given her for her golden wedding present—well, I am sure you see the point, Henry."

"Box guys ain't too bright," he said and rubbed his stony chin. Then he lifted his right thumb and bit it thoughtfully. He looked at the windows, at the corner of the room, at the floor. He looked at me from the corners of his eyes.

"Blackmail, huh?" he said. "Maybe. But crooks don't mix their rackets much. Still, the guy might pass the word along. There's a chance, Walter. I wouldn't care to hock my gold fillings to buy me a piece of it, but there's a chance. How much you figure to put out?"

"A hundred dollars should be ample, but I am willing to go as high as two hundred, which is the actual cost of the imitations."

Henry shook his head and patronized the bottle. "Nope. The guy wouldn't uncover hisself for that kind of money. Wouldn't be worth the chance he takes. He'd dump the marbles and keep his nose clean."

"We can at least try, Henry."

"Yeah, but where? And we're getting low on liquor. Maybe I better put my shoes on and run out, huh?"

At that very moment, as if in answer to my unspoken prayer, a soft dull thump sounded on the door of my apartment. I opened it and picked up the final edition of the evening paper. I closed the door again and carried the paper back across the room, opening it up as I went. I touched it with my right forefinger and smiled confidently at Henry Eichelberger.

"Here. I will wager you a full quart of Old Plantation that the answer will be on the crime page of this paper."

"There ain't any crime page," Henry chortled. "This is Los Angeles. I'll fade you."

I opened the paper to page three with some trepidation, for, although I had already seen the item I was looking for in an early edition of the paper while waiting in Ada Twomey's Domestic Employment Agency,

I was not certain it would appear intact in the later editions. But my faith was rewarded. It had not been removed, but appeared midway of column three exactly as before. The paragraph, which was quite short, was headed: LOU GANDESI QUESTIONED IN GEM THEFTS. "Listen to this, Henry," I said, and began to read.

> *Acting on an anonymous tip police late last night picked up Louis G. (Lou) Gandesi, proprietor of a well-known Spring Street tavern, and quizzed him intensively concerning the recent wave of dinner-party hold-ups in an exclusive western section of this city, hold-ups during which, it is alleged, more than two hundred thousand dollars' worth of valuable jewels have been torn at gun's point from women guests in fashionable homes. Gandesi was released at a late hour and refused to make any statement to reporters. "I never kibitz the cops," he said modestly. Captain William Norgaard, of the General Robbery Detail, announced himself as satisfied that Gandesi had no connection with the robberies, and that the tip was merely an act of personal spite.*

I folded the paper and threw it on the bed.

"You win, bo," Henry said, and handed me the bottel. I took a long drink and returned it to him. "Now what? Brace this Gandesi and take him through the hoops?"

"He may be a dangerous man, Henry. Do you think we are equal to it?"

Henry snorted contemptuously. "Yah, a Spring Street punk. Some fat slob with a phony ruby on his mitt. Lead me to him. We'll turn the slob inside out and drain his liver. But we're just about fresh out of liquor. All we got is maybe a pint." He examined the bottle against the light.

"We have had enough for the moment, Henry."

"We ain't drunk, are we? I only had seven drinks since I got here, maybe nine."

"Certainly we are not drunk, Henry, but you take very large drinks, and we have a difficult evening before us. I think we should now get shaved and dressed, and I further think that we should wear dinner clothes. I have an extra suit which will fit you admirably, as we are almost exactly the same size. It is certainly a remarkable omen that two such large men should be associated in the same enterprise. Evening clothes impress these low characters, Henry."

"Swell," Henry said. "They'll think we're mugs workin' for some big shot. This Gandesi will be scared enough to swallow his necktie."

We decided to do as I had suggested and I laid out clothes for Henry, and while he was bathing and shaving I telephoned to Ellen Macintosh.

"Oh, Walter, I am so glad you called up," she cried. "Have you found anything?"

"Not yet, darling," I said. "But we have an idea. Henry and I are just about to put it into execution."

"Henry, Walter? Henry who?"

"Why, Henry Eichelberger, of course, darling. Have you forgotten him so soon? Henry and I are warm friends and we—"

She interrupted me coldly. "Are you drinking, Walter?" she demanded in a very distant voice.

"Certainly not, darling. Henry is a teetotaler."

She sniffed sharply. I could hear the sound distinctly over the telephone. "But didn't Henry take the pearls?" she asked, after quite a long pause.

"Henry, angel? Of course not. Henry left because he was in love with you."

"Oh, Walter. That ape? I'm sure you're drinking terribly. I don't ever want to speak to you again. Goodbye." And she hung the phone up very sharply so that a painful sensation made itself felt in my ear.

I sat down in a chair with a bottle of Old Plantation in my hand wondering what I had said that could be construed as offensive or indiscreet. As I was unable to think of anything, I consoled myself with the bottle until Henry came out of the bathroom looking extremely personable in one of my pleated shirts and a wing collar and black bow tie.

It was dark when we left the apartment and I, at least, was full of hope and confidence, although a little depressed by the way Ellen Macintosh had spoken to me over the telephone.

## 4

Mr. Gandesi's establishment was not difficult to find, inasmuch as the first taxicab driver Henry yelled at on Spring Street directed us to it. It was called the Blue Lagoon and its interior was bathed in an unpleasant blue light. Henry and I entered it steadily, since we had consumed a partly solid meal at Mandy's Carribean Grotto before starting out to find Mr. Gandesi. Henry looked almost handsome in my second-best dinner suit, with a fringed white scarf hanging over his shoulder, a lightweight black felt hat on the back of his head (which was only a little larger than mine), and a bottle of whiskey in each of the side pockets of the summer overcoat he was wearing.

The bar of the Blue Lagoon was crowded, but Henry and I went on back to the small dim dining room behind it. A man in a dirty dinner suit came up to us and Henry asked him for Gandesi, and he pointed out a fat man who sat alone at a small table in the far corner of the room. We went that way.

The man sat with a small glass of red wine in front of him and slowly twisted a large green stone on his finger. He did not look up. There were no other chairs at the table, so Henry leaned on it with both elbows.

"You Gandesi?" he said.

The man did not look up even then. He moved his thick black eyebrows together and said in an absent voice: "Si. Yes."

"We got to talk to you in private," Henry told him. "Where we won't be disturbed."

Gandesi looked up now and there was extreme boredom in his flat black almond-shaped eyes. "So?" he asked and shrugged. "Eet ees about what?"

"About some pearls," Henry said. "Forty-nine on the string, matched and pink."

"You sell—or you buy?" Gandesi inquired and his chin began to shake up and down as if with amusement.

"Buy," Henry said.

The man at the table crooked his finger quietly and a very large waiter appeared at his side. "Ees dronk," he said lifelessly. "Put dees men out."

The waiter took hold of Henry's shoulder. Henry reached up carelessly and took hold of the waiter's hand and twisted it. The waiter's face in that bluish light turned some color I could not describe, but which was not at all healthy. He let out a low moan. Henry dropped the hand and said to me: "Put a C-note on the table."

I took my wallet out and extracted from it one of the two hundred-dollar bills I had taken the precaution to obtain from the cashier at the Chateau Moraine. Gandesi stared at the bill and made a gesture to the large waiter, who went away rubbing his hand and holding it tight against his chest.

"What for?" Gandesi asked.

"Five minutes of your time alone."

"Ees very fonny. O.K., I bite." Gandesi took the bill

and folded it neatly and put it in his vest pocket. Then he put both hands on the table and pushed himself heavily to his feet. He started to waddle away without looking at us.

Henry and I followed him among the crowded tables to the far side of the dining room and through a door in the wainscoting and then down a narrow dim hallway. At the end of this Gandesi opened a door into a lighted room and stood holding it for us, with a grave smile on his olive face. I went in first.

As Henry passed in front of Gandesi into the room the latter, with surprising agility, took a small shiny black leather club from his clothes and hit Henry on the head with it very hard. Henry sprawled forward on his hands and knees. Gandesi shut the door of the room very quickly for a man of his build and leaned against it with the small club in his left hand. Now, very suddenly, in his right hand appeared a short but heavy black revolver.

"Ees very fonny," he said politely, and chuckled to himself.

Exactly what happened then I did not see clearly. Henry was at one instant on his hands and knees with his back to Gandesi. In the next, or possibly even in the same instant, something swirled like a big fish in water and Gandesi grunted. I then saw that Henry's hard blond head was buried in Gandesi's stomach and that Henry's large hands held both of Gandesi's hairy wrists. Then Henry straightened his body to its full height and Gandesi was high up in the air balanced on top of Henry's head, his mouth strained wide open and his face a dark purple color. Then Henry shook himself, as it seemed, quite lightly, and Gandesi landed on his back on the floor with a terrible thud and lay gasping. Then a key turned in the door and Henry stood with his back to it, holding both the club and the

revolver in his left hand, and solicitously feeling the
pockets which contained our supply of whiskey. All
this happened with such rapidity that I leaned against
the side wall and felt a little sick at my stomach.

"A gut-buster," Henry drawled. "A comedian.
Wait'll I loosen my belt."

Gandesi rolled over and got to his feet very slowly
and painfully and stood swaying and passing his hand
up and down his face. His clothes were covered with
dust.

"This here's a sap," Henry said, showing me the
small black club. "He hit me with it, didn't he?"

"Why, Henry, don't you know?" I inquired.

"I just wanted to be sure," Henry said. "You don't
do that to the Eichelbergers."

"O.K., what you boys want?" Gandesi asked abruptly, with no trace whatever of his Italian accent.

"I told you what we wanted, dough-face."

"I don't think I know you boys," Gandesi said and
lowered his body with care into a wooden chair beside
a shabby office desk. He mopped his face and neck
and felt himself in various places.

"You got the wrong idea, Gandesi. A lady living in
Carondelet Park lost a forty-nine bead pearl necklace
a couple of days back. A box job, but a pushover.
Our outfit's carrying a little insurance on those marbles. And I'll take that *C* note."

He walked over to Gandesi and Gandesi quickly
reached the folded bill from his pocket and handed it to
him. Henry gave me the bill and I put it back in my
wallet.

"I don't think I hear about it," Gandesi said carefully.

"You hit me with a sap," Henry said. "Listen kind
of hard."

Gandesi shook his head and then winced. "I don't

back no petermen," he said, "nor no heist guys. You got me wrong."

"Listen hard," Henry said in a low voice. "You might hear something." He swung the small black club lightly in front of his body with two fingers of his right hand. The slightly too-small hat was still on the back of his head, although a little crumpled.

"Henry," I said, "you seem to be doing all the work this evening. Do you think that is quite fair?"

"O.K., work him over," Henry said. "These fat guys bruise something lovely."

By this time Gandesi had become a more natural color and was gazing at us steadily. "Insurance guys, huh?" he inquired dubiously.

"You said it, dough-face."

"You try Melachrino?" Gandesi asked.

"Haw," Henry began raucously, "a gut-buster. A—" but I interrupted him sharply.

"One moment, Henry," I said. Then turning to Gandesi, "Is this Melachrino a person?" I asked him.

Gandesi's eyes rounded in surprise. "Sure—a guy. You don't know him, huh?" A look of dark suspicion was born in his sloe-black eyes, but vanished almost as soon as it appeared.

"Phone him," Henry said, pointing to the instrument which stood on the shabby office desk.

"Phone is bad," Gandesi objected thoughtfully.

"So is sap poison," Henry said.

Gandesi sighed and turned his thick body in the chair and drew the telephone towards him. He dialed a number with an inky nail and listened. After an interval he said: "Joe? . . . Lou. Couple insurance guys tryin' to deal on a Carondelet Park job . . . Yeah . . . No, marbles . . . You ain't heard a whisper, huh? . . . O.K., Joe."

Gandesi replaced the phone and swung around in

the chair again. He studied us with sleepy eyes. "No soap. What insurance outfit you boys work for?"

"Give him a card," Henry said to me.

I took my wallet out once more and withdrew one of my cards from it. It was an engraved calling card and contained nothing but my name. So I used my pocket pencil to write, Chateau Moraine Apartments, Franklin near Ivar, below the name. I showed the card to Henry and then gave it to Gandesi.

Gandesi read the card and quietly bit his finger. His face brightened suddenly. "You boys better see Jack Lawler," he said.

Henry stared at him closely. Gandesi's eyes were now bright and unblinking and guileless.

"Who's he?" Henry asked.

"Runs the Penguin Club. Out on the Strip—Eighty-six Forty-four Sunset or some number like that. He can find out, if any guy can."

"Thanks," Henry said quietly. He glanced at me. "You believe him?"

"Well, Henry," I said, "I don't really think he would be above telling us an untruth."

"Haw!" Gandesi began suddenly. "A gut-buster! A—"

"Can it!" Henry snarled. "That's my line. Straight goods, is it, Gandesi? About this Jack Lawler?"

Gandesi nodded vigorously. "Straight goods, absolute. Jack Lawler got a finger in everything high class that's touched. But he ain't easy to see."

"Don't worry none about that. Thanks, Gandesi."

Henry tossed the black club into the corner of the room and broke open the breech of the revolver he had been holding all this time in his left hand. He ejected the shells and then bent down and slid the gun along the floor until it disappeared under the desk. He tossed the cartridges idly in his hand for a moment and then let them spill on the floor.

"So long, Gandesi," he said coldly. "And keep that schnozzle of yours clean, if you don't want to be looking for it under the bed."

He opened the door then and we both went out quickly and left the Blue Lagoon without interference from any of the employees.

## 5

My car was parked a short distance away down the block. We entered it and Henry leaned his arms on the wheel and stared moodily through the windshield.

"Well, what you think, Walter?" he inquired at length.

"If you ask my opinion, Henry, I think Mr. Gandesi told us a cock-and-bull story merely to get rid of us. Furthermore I do not believe he thought we were insurance agents."

"Me too, and an extra helping," Henry said. "I don't figure there's any such guy as this Melachrino or this Jack Lawler and this Gandesi called up some dead number and had himself a phony chin with it. I oughta go back there and pull his arms and legs off. The hell with the fat slob."

"We had the best idea we could think of, Henry, and we executed it to the best of our ability. I now suggest that we return to my apartment and try to think of something else."

"And get drunk," Henry said, starting the car and guiding it away from the curb.

"We could perhaps have a small allowance of liquor, Henry."

"Yah!" Henry snorted. "A stall. I oughta go back there and wreck the joint."

He stopped at the intersection, although no traffic signal was in operation at the time; and raised a bottle of whiskey to his lips. He was in the act of drinking when a car came up behind us and collided with our car, but not very severely. Henry choked and lowered his bottle, spilling some of the liquor on his garments.

"This town's getting too crowded," he snarled. "A guy can't take hisself a drink without some smart monkey bumps his elbow."

Whoever it was in the car behind us blew a horn with some insistence, inasmuch as our car had not yet moved forward. Henry wrenched the door open and got out and went back. I heard voices of considerable loudness, the louder being Henry's voice. He came back after a moment and got into the car and drove on.

"I oughta have pulled his mush off," he said, "but I went soft." He drove rapidly the rest of the way to Hollywood and the Chateau Moraine and we went up to my apartment and sat down with large glasses in our hands.

"We got better than a quart and a half of hooch," Henry said, looking at the two bottles which he had placed on the table beside others which had long since been emptied. "That oughta be good for an idea."

"If it isn't enough, Henry, there is an abundant further supply where it came from," I drained my glass cheerfully.

"You seem a right guy," Henry said. "What makes you always talk so funny?"

"I cannot seem to change my speech, Henry. My father and mother were both severe purists in the New England tradition, and the vernacular has never come naturally to my lips, even while I was in college."

Henry made an attempt to digest this remark, but I could see that it lay somewhat heavily on his stomach.

We talked for a time concerning Gandesi and the

doubtful quality of his advice, and thus passed perhaps half an hour. Then rather suddenly the white telephone on my desk began to ring. I hurried over to it, hoping that it was Ellen Macintosh and that she had recovered from her ill humor. But it proved to be a male voice and a strange one to me. It spoke crisply, with an unpleasant metallic quality of tone.

"You Walter Gage?"

"This is Mister Gage speaking."

"Well, *Mister* Gage, I understand you're in the market for some jewelry."

I held the phone very tightly and turned my body and made grimaces to Henry over the top of the instrument. But he was moodily pouring himself another large portion of Old Plantation.

"That is so," I said into the telephone, trying to keep my voice steady, although my excitement was almost too much for me. "If by jewelry you mean pearls."

"Forty-nine in a rope, brother. And five grand is the price."

"Why that is entirely absurd," I gasped. "Five thousand dollars for those—"

The voice broke in on me rudely. "You heard me, brother. Five grand. Just hold up the hand and count the fingers. No more, no less. Think it over. I'll call you later."

The phone clicked dryly and I replaced the instrument shakily in its cradle. I was trembling. I walked back to my chair and sat down and wiped my face with my handkerchief.

"Henry," I said in a low tense voice, "it worked. But how strangely."

Henry put his empty glass down on the floor. It was the first time that I had ever seen him put an empty glass down and leave it empty. He stared at me closely with his tight unblinking green eyes.

"Yeah?" he said gently. "What worked, kid?" He licked his lips slowly with the tip of his tongue.

"What we accomplished down at Gandesi's place, Henry. A man just called me on the telephone and asked me if I was in the market for pearls."

"Geez." Henry pursed his lips and whistled gently. "That damn dago had something after all."

"But the price is five thousand dollars, Henry. That seems beyond reasonable explanation."

"Huh?" Henry's eyes seemed to bulge as if they were about to depart from their orbits. "Five grand for them ringers? The guy's nuts. They cost two *C's,* you said. Bugs completely is what the guy is. Five grand? Why, for five grand I could buy me enough phony pearls to cover an elephant's caboose."

I could see that Henry seemed puzzled. He refilled our glasses silently and we stared at each other over them. "Well, what the heck can you do with that, Walter?" he asked after a long silence.

"Henry," I said firmly, "there is only one thing to do. It is true that Ellen Macintosh spoke to me in confidence, and as she did not have Mrs. Penruddock's express permission to tell me about the pearls, I suppose I should respect that confidence. But Ellen is now angry with me and does not wish to speak to me, for the reason that I am drinking whiskey in considerable quantities, although my speech and brain are still reasonably clear. This last is a very strange development and I think, in spite of everything, some close friend of the family should be consulted. Preferably of course, a man, someone of large business experience, and in addition to that a man who understands about jewels. There *is* such a man, Henry, and tomorrow morning I shall call upon him."

"Geez," Henry said. "You coulda said all that in nine words, bo. Who is this guy?"

"His name is Mr. Lansing Gallemore, and he is president of the Gallemore Jewelry Company on Seventh Street. He is a very old friend of Mrs. Penruddock—Ellen has often mentioned him—and is, in fact, the very man who procured for her the imitation pearls."

"But this guy will tip the bulls," Henry objected.

"I do not think so, Henry. I do not think he will do anything to embarrass Mrs. Penruddock in any way."

Henry shrugged. "Phonies are phonies," he said. "You can't make nothing else outa them. Not even no president of no jewelry store can't."

"Nevertheless, there must be a reason why so large a sum is demanded, Henry. The only reason that occurs to me is blackmail and, frankly, that is a little too much for me to handle alone, because I do not know enough about the background of the Penruddock family."

"Oke," Henry said, sighing. "If that's your hunch, you better follow it, Walter. And I better breeze on home and flop so as to be in good shape for the rough work, if any."

"You would not care to pass the night here, Henry?"

"Thanks, pal, but I'm O.K. back at the hotel. I'll just take this spare bottle of the tiger sweat to put me to sleep. I might happen to get a call from the agency in the A.M. and would have to brush my teeth and go after it. And I guess I better change my duds back to where I can mix with the common people."

So saying he went into the bathroom and in a short time emerged wearing his own blue serge suite. I urged him to take my car, but he said it would not be safe in his neighborhood. He did, however, consent to use the topcoat he had been wearing and, placing in it carefully the unopened quart of whiskey, he shook me warmly by the hand.

"One moment, Henry," I said and took out my wallet. I extended a twenty-dollar bill to him.

"What's that in favor of?" he growled.

"You are temporarily out of employment, Henry, and you have done a noble piece of work this evening, puzzling as are the results. You should be rewarded and I can well afford this small token."

"Well, thanks, pal," Henry said. "But it's just a loan." His voice was gruff with emotion. "Should I give you a buzz in the A.M.?"

"By all means. And there is one thing more that has occurred to me. Would it not be advisable for you to change your hotel? Suppose, through no fault of mine, the police learn of this theft. Would they not at least suspect you?"

"Hell, they'd bounce me up and down for hours," Henry said. "But what'll it get them? I ain't no ripe peach."

"It is for you to decide, of course, Henry."

"Yeah. Good night, pal, and don't have no nightmares."

He left me then and I felt suddenly very depressed and lonely. Henry's company had been very stimulating to me, in spite of his rough way of talking. He was very much of a man. I poured myself a rather large drink of whiskey from the remaining bottle and drank it quickly but gloomily.

The effect was such that I had an overmastering desire to speak to Ellen Macintosh at all costs. I went to the telephone and called her number. After a long wait a sleepy maid answered. But Ellen, upon hearing my name, refused to come to the telephone. That depressed me still further and I finished the rest of the whiskey almost without noticing what I was doing. I then lay down on the bed and fell into fitful slumber.

## 6

The busy ringing of the telephone awoke me and I saw that the morning sunlight was streaming into the room. It was nine o'clock and all the lamps were still burning. I arose feeling a little stiff and dissipated, for I was still wearing my dinner suit. But I am a healthy man with very steady nerves and I did not feel as badly as I expected. I went to the telephone and answered it.

Henry's voice said: "How you feel, pal? I got a hangover like twelve Swedes."

"Not too badly, Henry."

"I got a call from the agency about a job. I better go down and take a gander at it. Should I drop around later?"

"Yes, Henry, by all means do that. By eleven o'clock I should be back from the errand about which I spoke to you last night."

"Any more calls from you know?"

"Not yet, Henry."

"Check. Abyssinia." He hung up and I took a cold shower and shaved and dressed. I donned a quiet brown business suit and had some coffee sent up from the coffee shop downstairs. I also had the waiter remove the empty bottles from my apartment and gave him a dollar for his trouble. After drinking two cups of black coffee I felt my own man once more and drove downtown to the Gallemore Jewelry Company's large and brilliant store on West Seventh Street.

It was another bright, golden morning and it seemed that somehow things should adjust themselves on so pleasant a day.

Mr. Lansing Gallemore proved to be a little difficult to see, so that I was compelled to tell his secretary that it was a matter concerning Mrs. Penruddock and of a confidential nature. Upon this message being carried in to him I was at once ushered into a long paneled office, at the far end of which Mr. Gallemore stood behind a massive desk. He extended a thin pink hand to me.

"Mr. Gage? I don't believe we have met, have we?"

"No, Mr. Gallemore, I do not believe we have. I am the fiancé—or was until last night—of Miss Ellen Macintosh, who, as you probably know, is Mrs. Penruddock's nurse. I am come to you upon a very delicate matter and it is necessary that I ask for your confidence before I speak."

He was a man of perhaps seventy-five years of age, and very thin and tall and correct and well preserved. He had cold blue eyes but a warming smile. He was attired youthfully enough in a gray flannel suit with a red carnation at his lapel.

"That is something I make it a rule never to promise, Mr. Gage," he said. "I think it is almost always a very unfair request. But if you assure me the matter concerns Mrs. Penruddock and is really of a delicate and confidential nature, I will make an exception."

"It is indeed, Mr. Gallemore," I said, and thereupon told him the entire story, concealing nothing, not even the fact that I had consumed far too much whiskey the day before.

He stared at me curiously at the end of my story. His finely shaped hand picked up an old-fashioned white quill pen and he slowly tickled his right ear with the feather of it.

"Mr. Gage," he said, "can't you guess why they ask five thousand dollars for that string of pearls?"

"If you permit me to guess, in a matter of so personal a nature, I could perhaps hazard an explanation, Mr. Gallemore."

He moved the white feather around to his left ear and nodded. "Go ahead, son."

"The pearls are in fact real, Mr. Gallemore. You are a very old friend of Mrs. Penruddock—perhaps even a childhood sweetheart. When she gave you her pearls, her golden wedding present, to sell because she was in sore need of money for a generous purpose, you did not sell them, Mr. Gallemore. You only pretended to sell them. You gave her twenty thousand dollars of your own money, and you returned the real pearls to her, pretending that they were an imitation made in Czechoslovakia."

"Son, you think a lot smarter than you talk," Mr. Gallemore said. He arose and walked to a window, pulled aside a fine net curtain and looked down on the bustle of Seventh Street. He came back to his desk and seated himself and smiled a little wistfully.

"You are almost embarrassingly correct, Mr. Gage," he said, and sighed. "Mrs. Penruddock is a very proud woman, or I should simply have offered her the twenty thousand dollars as an unsecured loan. I happened to be the coadministrator of Mr. Penruddock's estate and I knew that in the condition of the financial market at that time it would be out of the question to raise enough cash, without damaging the corpus of the estate beyond reason, to care for all those relatives and pensioners. So Mrs. Penruddock sold her pearls—as she thought—but she insisted that no one should know about it. And I did what you have guessed. It was unimportant. I could afford the gesture. I have never married, Gage, and I am rated a wealthy man. As a matter of fact, at that time, the pearls would not have fetched more than half of what I gave her, or of what they should bring today."

I lowered my eyes for fear this kindly old gentleman might be troubled by my direct gaze.

"So I think we had better raise that five thousand, son," Mr. Gallemore at once added in a brisk voice.

"The price is pretty low, although stolen pearls are a great deal more difficult to deal in than cut stones. If I should care to trust you that far on your face, do you think you could handle the assignment?"

"Mr. Gallemore," I said firmly but quietly, "I am a total stranger to you and I am only flesh and blood. But I promise you by the memories of my dead and revered parents that there will be no cowardice."

"Well, there is a good deal of the flesh and blood, son," Mr. Gallemore said kindly. "And I am not afraid of your stealing the money, because possibly I know a little more about Miss Ellen Macintosh and her boy friend than you might suspect. Furthermore, the pearls are insured, in my name, of course, and the insurance company should really handle this affair. But you and your funny friend seem to have got along very nicely so far, and I believe in playing out a hand. This Henry must be quite a man."

"I have grown very attached to him, in spite of his uncouth ways," I said.

Mr. Gallemore played with his white quill pen a little longer and then he brought out a large checkbook and wrote a check, which he carefully blotted and passed across the desk.

"If you get the pearls, I'll see that the insurance people refund this to me," he said. "If they like my business, there will be no difficulty about that. The bank is down at the corner and I will be waiting for their call. They won't cash the check without telephoning me, probably. Be careful, son, and don't get hurt."

He shook hands with me once more and I hesitated. "Mr. Gallemore, you are placing a greater trust in me than any man ever has," I said. "With the exception, of course, of my own father."

"I am acting like a damn fool," he said with a peculiar smile. "It is so long since I heard anyone talk the way Jane Austen writes that it is making a sucker out of me."

"Thank you, sir. I know my language is a bit stilted. Dare I ask you to do me a small favor, sir?"

"What is it, Gage?"

"To telephone Miss Ellen Macintosh, from whom I am now a little estranged, and tell her that I am not drinking today, and that you have entrusted me with a very delicate mission."

He laughed aloud. "I'll be glad to, Walter. And as I know she can be trusted, I'll give her an idea of what's going on."

I left him then and went down to the bank with the check, and the teller, after looking at me suspiciously, then absenting himself from his cage for a long time, finally counted out the money in hundred-dollar bills with the reluctance one might have expected, if it had been his own money.

I placed the flat packet of bills in my pocket and said: "Now give me a roll of quarters, please."

"A roll of quarters, sir?" His eyebrows lifted.

"Exactly. I use them for tips. And naturally I should prefer to carry them home in the wrappings."

"Oh, I see. Ten dollars, please."

I took the fat hard roll of coins and dropped it into my pocket and drove back to Hollywood.

Henry was waiting for me in the lobby of the Chateau Moraine, twirling his hat between his rough hard hands. His face looked a little more deeply lined than it had the day before and I noticed that his breath smelled of whiskey. We went up to my apartment and he turned to me eagerly.

"Any luck, pal?"

"Henry," I said, "before we proceed further into this day I wish it clearly understood that I am not drinking. I see that already you have been at the bottle."

"Just a pick-up, Walter," he said a little contritely. "That job I went out for was gone before I got there. What's the good word?"

I sat down and lit a cigarette and stared at him evenly. "Well, Henry, I don't really know whether I should tell you or not. But it seems a little petty not to do so after all you did last night to Gandesi." I hesitated a moment longer while Henry stared at me and pinched the muscles of his left arm. "The pearls are real, Henry. And I have instructions to proceed with the business and I have five thousand dollars in cash in my pocket at this moment."

I told him briefly what had happened.

He was more amazed than words could tell. "Cripes!" he exclaimed, his mouth hanging wide open. "You mean you got the five grand from this Gallemore —just like that?"

"Precisely that, Henry."

"Kid," he said earnestly, "you got something with that daisy pan and that fluff talk that a lot of guys would give important dough to cop. Five grand—out of a business guy—just like that. Why, I'll be a monkey's uncle. I'll be a snake's daddy. I'll be a mickey finn at a woman's-club lunch."

At that exact moment, as if my entrance to the building had been observed, the telephone rang again and I sprang to answer it.

It was one of the voices I was awaiting, but not the one I wanted to hear with the greater longing. "How's it looking to you this morning, Gage?"

"It is looking better," I said. "If I can have any assurance of honorable treatment, I am prepared to go through with it."

"You mean you got the dough?"

"In my pocket at this exact moment."

The voice seemed to exhale a slow breath. "You'll

get your marbles O.K.—if we get the price, Gage. We're in this business for a long time and we don't welsh. If we did, it would soon get around and nobody would play with us any more."

"Yes, I can readily understand that," I said. "Proceed with your instructions," I added coldly.

"Listen close, Gage. Tonight at eight sharp you be in Pacific Palisades. Know where that is?"

"Certainly. It is a small residential section west of the polo fields on Sunset Boulevard."

"Right. Sunset goes slap through it. There's one drugstore there—open till nine. Be there waiting a call at eight sharp tonight. Alone. And I mean alone, Gage. No cops and no strong-arm guys. It's rough country down there and we got a way to get you to where we want you and know if you're alone. Get all this?"

"I am not entirely an idiot," I retorted.

"No dummy packages, Gage. The dough will be checked. No guns. You'll be searched and there's enough of us to cover you from all angles. We know your car. No funny business, no smart work, no slip-up and nobody hurt. That's the way we do business. How's the dough fixed?"

"One-hundred-dollar bills," I said. "And only a few of them are new."

"Attaboy. Eight o'clock then. Be smart, Gage."

The phone clicked in my ear and I hung up. It rang again almost instantly. This time it was the *one* voice.

"Oh, Walter," Ellen cried, "I was so mean to you! Please forgive me, Walter. Mr. Gallemore has told me everything and I'm so frightened."

"There is nothing of which to be frightened," I told her warmly. "Does Mrs. Penruddock know, darling?"

"No, darling. Mr. Gallemore told me not to tell her. I am phoning from a store down on Sixth Street. Oh,

Walter, I really am frightened. Will Henry go with you?"

"I am afraid not, darling. The arrangements are all made and they will not permit it. I must go alone."

"Oh, Walter! I'm terrified. I can't bear the suspense."

"There is nothing to fear," I assured her. "It is a simple business transaction. And I am not exactly a midget."

"But, Walter—oh, I *will* try to be brave, Walter. Will you promise me just one teensy-weensy little thing?"

"Not a drop, darling," I said firmly. "Not a single solitary drop."

"Oh, Walter!"

There was a little more of that sort of thing, very pleasant to me in the circumstances, although possibly not of great interest to others. We finally parted with my promise to telephone as soon as the meeting between the crooks and myself had been consummated.

I turned from the telephone to find Henry drinking deeply from a bottle he had taken from his hip pocket.

"Henry!" I cried sharply.

He looked at me over the bottle with a shaggy determined look. "Listen, pal," he said in a low hard voice. "I got enough of your end of the talk to figure the set-up. Some place out in the tall weeds and you go alone and they feed you the old sap poison and take your dough and leave you lying—with the marbles still in their kitty. Nothing doing, pal. I said—nothing doing!" He almost shouted the last words.

"Henry, it is my duty and I must do it," I said quietly.

"Haw!" Henry snorted. "I say no. You're a nut, but you're a sweet guy on the side. I say no. Henry Eichelberger of the Wisconsin Eichelbergers—in fact, I might just as leave say of the Milwaukee Eichelbergers—says no. And he says it with both hands working." He drank again from his bottle.

"You certainly will not help matters by becoming intoxicated," I told him rather bitterly.

He lowered the bottle and looked at me with amazement written all over his rugged features. "Drunk, Walter?" he boomed. "Did I hear you say drunk? An Eichelberger drunk? Listen, son. We ain't got a lot of time now. It would take maybe three months. Some day when you got three months and maybe five thousand gallons of whiskey and a funnel, I would be glad to take my own time and show you what an Eichelberger looks like when drunk. You wouldn't believe it. Son, there wouldn't be nothing left of this town but a few sprung girders and a lot of busted bricks, in the middle of which—Geez, I'll get talking English myself if I hang around you much longer—in the middle of which, peaceful, with no human life nearer than maybe fifty miles, Henry Eichelberger will be on his back smiling at the sun. Drunk, Walter. Not stinking drunk, not even country-club drunk. But you could use the word drunk and I wouldn't take no offense."

He sat down and drank again. I stared moodily at the floor. There was nothing for me to say.

"But that," Henry said, "is some other time. Right now I am just taking my medicine. I ain't myself without a slight touch of delirium tremens, as the guy says. I was brought up on it. And I'm going with you, Walter. Where is this place at?"

"It's down near the beach, Henry, and you are not going with me. If you must get drunk—get drunk, but you are not going with me."

"You got a big car, Walter. I'll hide in back on the floor under a rug. It's a cinch."

"No, Henry."

"Walter, you are a sweet guy," Henry said, "and I

am going with you into this frame. Have a smell from the barrel, Walter. You look to me kind of frail."

We argued for an hour and my head ached and I began to feel very nervous and tired. It was then that I made what might have been a fatal mistake. I succumbed to Henry's blandishments and took a small portion of whiskey, purely for medicinal purposes. This made me feel so much more relaxed that I took another and larger portion. I had had no food except coffee that morning and only a very light dinner the evening before. At the end of another hour Henry had been out for two more bottles of whiskey and I was as bright as a bird. All difficulties had now disappeared and I had agreed heartily that Henry should lie in the back of my car hidden by a rug and accompany me to the rendezvous.

We had passed the time very pleasantly until two o'clock, at which hour I began to feel sleepy and lay down on the bed, and fell into a deep slumber.

# 7

When I awoke again it was almost dark. I rose from the bed with panic in my heart, and also a sharp shoot of pain through my temples. It was only six-thirty, however. I was alone in the apartment and lengthening shadows were stealing across the floor. The display of empty whiskey bottles on the table was very disgusting. Henry Eichelberger was nowhere to be seen. With an instinctive pang, of which I was almost immediately ashamed, I hurried to my jacket hanging on the back of a chair and plunged my hand into the inner breast pocket. The packet of bills was there intact. After a brief hesitation, and with a feeling of secret guilt, I drew them out and slowly counted them over. Not a bill was missing. I replaced the money and tried to smile at myself for this lack of trust, and then switched on a light and went into the bathroom to take alternate hot and cold showers until my brain was once more comparatively clear.

I had done this and was dressing in fresh linen when a key turned in the lock and Henry Eichelberger entered with two wrapped bottles under his arm. He looked at me with what I thought was genuine affection.

"A guy that can sleep it off like you is a real champ, Walter," he said admiringly. "I snuck your keys so as not to wake you. I had to get some eats and some more hooch. I done a little solo drinking, which as I told you is against my principles, but this is a big day. However, we take it easy from now on as to the hooch. We can't afford no jitters till it's all over."

He had unwrapped a bottle while he was speaking and poured me a small drink. I drank it gratefully and immediately felt a warm glow in my veins.

"I bet you looked in your poke for that deck of mazuma," Henry said, grinning at me.

I felt myself reddening, but I said nothing. "O.K., pal, you done right. What the heck do you know about Henry Eichelberger anyways? I done something else." He reached behind him and drew a short automatic from his hip pocket. "If these boys wanta play rough," he said, "I got me five bucks worth of iron that don't mind playin' rough a little itself. And the Eichelbergers ain't missed a whole lot of the guys they shot at."

"I don't like that, Henry," I said severely. "That is contrary to the agreement."

"Nuts to the agreement," Henry said. "The boys get their dough and no cops. I'm out to see that they hand over them marbles and don't pull any fast footwork."

I saw there was no use arguing with him, so I completed my dressing and prepared to leave the apart-

ment. We each took one more drink and then Henry
put a full bottle in his pocket and we left.

On the way down the hall to the elevator he ex-
plained in a low voice: "I got a hack out front to tail
you, just in case these boys got the same idea. You
might circle a few quiet blocks so as I can find out.
More like they don't pick you up till down close to the
beach."

"All this must be costing you a great deal of money,
Henry," I told him, and while we were waiting for the
elevator to come up I took another twenty-dollar bill
from my wallet and offered it to him. He took the
money reluctantly, but finally folded it and placed it in
his pocket.

I did as Henry had suggested, driving up and down a
number of the hilly streets north of Hollywood Boulevard, and presently I heard the unmistakable hoot of a
taxicab horn behind me. I pulled over to the side of the
road. Henry got out of the cab and paid off the driver
and got into my car beside me.

"All clear," he said. "No tail. I'll just keep kind of
slumped down and you better stop somewhere for some
groceries on account of if we have to get rough with
these mugs, a full head of steam will help."

So I drove westward and dropped down to Sunset
Boulevard and presently stopped at a crowded drive-in
restaurant where we sat at the counter and ate a light
meal of omelette and black coffee. We then proceeded
on our way. When we reached Beverly Hills, Henry
again made me wind in and out through a number of
residential streets where he observed very carefully
through the rear window of the car.

Fully satisfied at last we drove back to Sunset, and
without incident onwards through Bel-Air and the
fringes of Westwood, almost as far as the Riviera Polo
field. At this point, down in the hollow, there is a can-

yon called Mandeville Canyon, a very quiet place. Henry had me drive up this for a short distance. We then stopped and had a little whiskey from his bottle and he climbed into the back of the car and curled his big body up on the floor, with the rug over him and his automatic pistol and his bottle down on the floor conveniently to his hand. That done I once more resumed my journey.

Pacific Palisades is a district whose inhabitants seem to retire rather early. When I reached what might be called the business center nothing was open but the drugstore beside the bank. I parked the car, with Henry remaining silent under the rug in the back, except for a slight gurgling noise I noticed as I stood on the dark sidewalk. Then I went into the drugstore and saw by its clock that it was now fifteen minutes to eight. I bought a package of cigarettes and lit one and took up my position near the open telephone booth.

The druggist, a heavy-set red-faced man of uncertain age, had a small radio up very loud and was listening to some foolish serial. I asked him to turn it down, as I was expecting an important telephone call. This he did, but not with any good grace, and immediately retired to the back part of his store whence I saw him looking out at me malignantly through a small glass window.

At precisely one minute to eight by the drugstore clock the phone rang sharply in the booth. I hastened into it and pulled the door tight shut. I lifted the receiver, trembling a little in spite of myself.

It was the same cool metallic voice. "Gage?"

"This is Mr. Gage."

"You done just what I told you?"

"Yes," I said. "I have the money in my pocket and I am entirely alone." I did not like the feeling of lying so brazenly, even to a thief, but I steeled myself to it.

"Listen, then. Go back about three hundred feet the

way you come. Beside the firehouse there's a service
station, closed up, painted green and red and white.
Beside that, going south, is a dirt road. Follow it three
quarters of a mile and you come to a white fence of
four-by-four built almost across the road. You can just
squeeze your car by at the left side. Dim your lights
and get through there and keep going down the little
hill into a hollow with sage all around. Park there, cut
your lights, and wait. Get it?"

"Perfectly," I said coldly, "and it shall be done exactly that way."

"And listen, pal. There ain't a house in half a mile,
and there ain't any folks around at all. You got ten
minutes to get there. You're watched right this minute.
You get there fast and you get there alone—or you got
a trip for biscuits. And don't light no matches or pills
nor use no flashlights. On your way."

The phone went dead and I left the booth. I was
scarcely outside the drugstore before the druggist
rushed at his radio and turned it up to a booming
blare. I got into my car and turned it and drove back
along Sunset Boulevard, as directed. Henry was as still
as the grave on the floor behind me.

I was now very nervous and Henry had all the liquor
which we had brought with us. I reached the firehouse
in no time at all and through its front window I
could see four firemen playing cards. I turned to the
right down the dirt road past the red-and-green-and-
white service station and almost at once the night was
so still, in spite of the quiet sound of my car, that I
could hear the crickets and treefrogs chirping and trill-
ing in all directions, and from some nearby watery spot
came the hoarse croak of a solitary bullfrog.

The road dipped and rose again and far off there was
a yellow window. Then ahead of me, ghostly in the
blackness of the moonless night, appeared the dim

white barrier across the road. I noted the gap at the side and them dimmed my headlamps and steered carefully through it and so on down a rough short hill into an oval-shaped hollow space surrounded by low brush and plentifully littered with empty bottles and cans and pieces of paper. It was entirely deserted, however, at this dark hour. I stopped my car and shut off the ignition, and the lights, and sat there motionless, hands on the wheel.

Behind me I heard no murmur of sound from Henry. I waited possibly five minutes, although it seemed much longer, but nothing happened. It was very still, very lonely, and I did not feel happy.

Finally there was a faint sound of movement behind me and I looked back to see the pale blur of Henry's face peering at me from under the rug.

His voice whispered huskily. "Anything stirring, Walter?"

I shook my head at him vigorously and he once more pulled the rug over his face. I heard a faint sound of gurgling.

Fully fifteen minutes passed before I dared to move again. By this time the tensity of waiting had made me stiff. I therefore boldly unlatched the door of the car and stepped out upon the rough ground. Nothing happened. I walked slowly back and forth with my hands in my pockets. More and more time dragged by. More than half an hour had now elapsed and I became impatient. I went to the rear window of the car and spoke softly into the interior.

"Henry, I fear we have been victimized in a very cheap way. I fear very much that this is nothing but a low practical joke on the part of Mr. Gandesi in retaliation for the way you handled him last night. There is no one here and only one possible way of arriving.

It looks to me like a very unlikely place for the sort of meeting we have been expecting."

"The son of a bitch!" Henry whispered back, and the gurgling sound was repeated in the darkness of the car. Then there was movement and he appeared free of the rug. The door opened against my body. Henry's head emerged. He looked in all directions his eyes could command. "Sit down on the running board," he whispered. "I'm getting out. If they got a bead on us from them bushes, they'll only see one head."

I did what Henry suggested and turned my collar up high and pulled my hat down over my eyes. As noiselessly as a shadow Henry stepped out of the car and shut the door without sound and stood before me ranging the limited horizon with his eyes. I could see the dim reflection of light on the gun in his hand. We remained thus for ten more minutes.

Henry then got angry and threw discretion to the winds. "Suckered!" he snarled. "You know what happened, Walter?"

"No, Henry. I do not."

"It was just a tryout, that's what it was. Somewhere along the line these dirty-so-and-so's checked on you to see did you play ball, and then again they checked on you at that drugstore back there. I bet you a pair of solid platinum bicycle wheels that was a long-distance call you caught back there."

"Yes, Henry, now that you mention it, I am sure it was," I said sadly.

"There you are, kid. The bums ain't even left town. They are sitting back there beside their plush-lined spittoons giving you the big razzoo. And tomorrow this guy calls you again on the phone and says O.K. so far, but they had to be careful and they will try again to-night maybe out in San Fernando Valley and the price will be upped to ten grand, on account of their extra trouble. I oughta go back there and twist that Gandesi so he would be lookin' up his left pants leg."

"Well, Henry," I said, "after all, I did not do exactly what they told me to, because you insisted on coming with me. And perhaps they are more clever than you think. So I think the best thing now is to go back to town and hope there will be a chance tomorrow to try again. And you must promise me faithfully not to interfere."

"Nuts!" Henry said angrily. "Without me along they would take you the way the cat took the canary. You are a sweet guy, Walter, but you don't know as many answers as Baby Leroy. These guys are thieves and they have a string of marbles that might probably bring them twenty grand with careful handling. They are out for a quick touch, but they will squeeze all they can just the same. I oughta go back to that fat wop Gandesi right now. I could do things to that slob that ain't been invented yet."

"Now, Henry, don't get violent," I said.

"Haw," Henry snarled. "Them guys give me an ache in the back of my lap." He raised his bottle to his lips with his left hand and drank thirstily. His voice came down a few tones and sounded more peaceful. "Better dip the bill, Walter. The party's a flop."

"Perhaps you are right, Henry," I sighed. "I will admit that my stomach has been trembling like an autumn leaf for all of half an hour."

So I stood up boldly beside him and poured a liberal portion of the fiery liquid down my throat. At once my courage revived. I handed the bottle back to Henry and he placed it carefully down on the running board. He stood beside me dancing the short automatic pistol up and down on the broad palm of his hand.

"I don't need no tools to handle that bunch. The hell with it." And with a sweep of his arm he hurled the pistol off among the bushes, where it fell to the ground with a muffled thud. He walked away from the car and stood with his arms akimbo, looking up at the sky.

I moved over beside him and watched his averted face, insofar as I was able to see it in that dim light. A strange melancholy came over me. In the brief time I had known Henry I had grown very fond of him.

"Well, Henry," I said at last, "what is the next move?"

"Beat it on home, I guess," he said slowly and mournfully. "And get good and drunk." He doubled his hands into fists and shook them slowly. Then he turned to face me. "Yeah," he said. "Nothing else to do. Beat it on home, kid, is all that is left to us."

"Not quite yet, Henry," I said softly.

I took my right hand out of my pocket. I have large hands. In my right hand nestled the roll of wrapped quarters which I had obtained at the bank that morning. My hand made a large fist around them.

"Good night, Henry," I said quietly, and swung my fist with all the weight of my arm and body. "You had two strikes on me, Henry," I said. "The big one is still left."

But Henry was not listening to me. My fist with the wrapped weight of metal inside it had caught him fairly and squarely on the point of his jaw. His legs became boneless and he pitched straight forward, brushing my sleeve as he fell. I stepped quickly out of his way.

Henry Eichelberger lay motionless on the ground, as limp as a rubber glove.

I looked down at him a little sadly, waiting for him to stir, but he did not move a muscle. He lay inert, completely unconscious. I dropped the roll of quarters back into my pocket, bent over him, searched him thoroughly, moving him around like a sack of meal, but it was a long time before I found the pearls. They were twined around his ankle inside his left sock.

"Well, Henry," I said, speaking to him for the last time, although he could not hear me, "you are a gentleman, even if you are a thief. You could have taken the money a dozen times this afternoon and given me nothing. You could have taken it a little while ago when you had the gun in your hand, but even that repelled you. You threw the gun away and we were man to man, far from help, far from interference. And even then you hesitated, Henry. In fact, Henry, I think for a successful thief you hesitated just a little too long. But as a man of sporting feelings I can only think the more highly of you. Goodbye, Henry, and good luck."

I took my wallet out and withdrew a one-hundred-dollar bill and placed it carefully in the pocket where I had seen Henry put his money. Then I went back to the car and took a drink out of the whiskey bottle and corked it firmly and laid it beside him, convenient to his right hand.

I felt sure that when he awakened he would need it.

# 8

It was past ten o'clock when I returned home to my apartment, but I at once went to the telephone and called Ellen Macintosh. "Darling!" I cried. "I have the pearls."

I caught the sound of her indrawn breath over the wire. "Oh darling," she said tensely and excitedly, "and you are not hurt? They did not hurt you, darling? They just took the money and let you go?"

"There were no 'they,' darling," I said proudly. "I

still have Mr. Gallemore's money intact. There was only Henry."

"Henry!" she cried in a very strange voice. "But I thought—Come over here at once, Walter Gage, and tell me—"

"I have whiskey on my breath, Ellen."

"Darling! I'm sure you needed it. Come at once."

So once more I went down to the street and hurried to Carondelet Park and in no time at all was at the Penruddock residence. Ellen came out on the porch to meet me and we talked there quietly in the dark, holding hands, for the household had gone to bed. As simple as I could I told her my story.

"But darling," she said at last, "how did you know it was Henry? I thought Henry was your friend. And this other voice on the telephone—"

"Henry *was* my friend," I said a little sadly, "and that is what destroyed him. As to the voice on the telephone, that was a small matter and easily arranged. Henry was away from me a number of times to arrange it. There was just one small point that gave me thought. After I gave Gandesi my private card with the name of my apartment house scribbled upon it, it was necessary for Henry to communicate to his confederate that we had seen Gandesi and given him my name and address. For of course when I had this foolish, or perhaps not so very foolish idea of visiting some well-known underworld character in order to send a message that we would buy back the pearls, this was Henry's opportunity to make me think the telephone message came as a result of our talking to Gandesi, and telling him our difficulty. But since the first call came to me at my apartment before Henry had had a chance to inform his confederate of our meeting with Gandesi, it was obvious that a trick had been employed.

"Then I recalled that a car had bumped into us

from behind and Henry had gone back to abuse the driver. And of course the bumping was deliberate, and Henry had made the opportunity for it on purpose, and his confederate was in the car. So Henry, while pretending to shout at him, was able to convey the necessary information."

"But, Walter," Ellen said, having listened to his explanation a little impatiently, "that is a very small matter. What I really want to know is how you decided that Henry had the pearls at all."

"But you told me he had them," I said. "You were quite sure of it. Henry is a very durable character. It would be just like him to hide the pearls somewhere, having no fear of what the police might do to him, and get another position and then after perhaps quite a long time, retrieve the pearls and quietly leave this part of the country."

Ellen shook her head impatiently in the darkness of the porch. "Walter," she said sharply, "you are hiding something. You could not have been sure and you would not have hit Henry in that brutal way, unless you had been sure. I know you well enough to know that."

"Well, darling," I said modestly, "there was indeed another small indication, one of those foolish trifles which the cleverest men overlook. As you know, I do not use the regular apartment-house telephone, not wishing to be annoyed by solicitors and such people. The phone which I use is a private line and its number is unlisted. But the calls I received from Henry's confederate came over that phone, and Henry had been in my apartment a great deal, and I had been careful not to give Mr. Gandesi that number, because of course I did not expect anything from Mr. Gandesi, as I was perfectly sure from the beginning that Henry had the pearls, if only I could get him to bring them out of hiding."

"Oh, darling," Ellen cried, and threw her arms around me. "How brave you are, and I really think that you are actually clever in your own peculiar way. Do you believe that Henry was in love with me?"

But that was a subject in which I had no interest whatever. I left the pearls in Ellen's keeping and late as the hour now was I drove at once to the residence of Mr. Lansing Gallemore and told him my story and gave him back his money.

A few months later I was happy to receive a letter postmarked in Honolulu and written on a very inferior brand of paper.

*Well, pal, that Sunday punch of yours was the money and I did not think you had it in you, altho of course I was not set for it. But it was a pip and made me think of you for a week every time I brushed my teeth. It was too bad I had to scram because you are a sweet guy altho a little on the goofy side and I'd like to be getting plastered with you right now instead of wiping oil valves where I am at which is not where this letter is mailed by several thousand miles. There is just two things I would like you to know and they are both kosher. I did fall hard for that tall blonde and this was the main reason I took my time from the old lady. Glomming the pearls was just one of those screwy ideas a guy can get when he is dizzy with a dame. It was a crime the way they left them marbles lying around in that bread box and I worked for a Frenchy once in Djibouty and got to know pearls enough to tell them from snowballs. But when it came to the clinch down there in that brush with us two alone and no holds barred I just was too soft to go through with the deal. Tell that blonde you got a loop on I was asking for her.*

Yrs. *as ever,*

Henry Eichelberger (*Alias*)
*P.S. What do you know, that punk that did the phone*

*work on you tried to take me for a fifty cut on that
C note you tucked in my vest. I had to twist the
sucker plenty.*

*Yrs.* H. E. *(Alias)*